TRIP TO THE NORTH POLE

THE POLAR EXPRESS

TRIP TO THE NORTH POLE

ADAPTED
BY
ELLEN WEISS

BASED ON THE MOTION PICTURE SCREENPLAY
BY
**ROBERT ZEMECKIS
AND WILLIAM BROYLES, JR.**

BASED ON THE BOOK *THE POLAR EXPRESS*,
WRITTEN AND ILLUSTRATED
BY
CHRIS VAN ALLSBURG

DESIGN
BY
DOYLE PARTNERS

HOUGHTON MIFFLIN COMPANY, BOSTON 2004

www.polarexpress.com
www.polarexpressmovie.com

Library of Congress Cataloging-in-Publication Data
Weiss, Ellen, 1949–
Trip to the north / by Ellen Weiss.
p. cm.
"The Polar Express."
"Based on the motion picture screenplay by Robert Zemeckis and
William Broyles, Jr.; based on the book The Polar Express written
and illustrated by Chris Van Allsburg."
Summary: On Christmas Eve, a young boy joins some other
children on a magical train ride to the North Pole.
ISBN 0-618-47790-X
[1. Christmas—Fiction. 2. Railroads—Trains—Fiction. 3. Santa Claus—Fic-
tion. 4. North Pole—Fiction.] I. Zemeckis, Robert, 1952– II. Broyles, William.
III. Van Allsburg, Chris. IV. Title.
PZ7.W4472Tr 2004
[Fic]—dc22   2004007574

Manufactured in the United States of America
QUM 10 9 8 7 6 5 4 3 2 1

CONTENTS

1.

ON Christmas Eve, a Boy lay quietly in his bed. He did not rustle the sheets. He breathed slowly and silently, in and out, in and out, listening for a sound he never really thought he would hear: the ringing bells of Santa's sleigh.

The Boy's eyes flew open. *Was that it?* It was very faint, but he was sure he'd heard it — the distant jingling of a solitary sleigh bell. He sat up in bed and listened intently.

Nothing. There was only the ticking of his alarm clock.

Quietly, the Boy slipped out from under his Roy Rogers sheets and tiptoed to the window in his yellow flannel pajamas. Leaning over the steam radiator, he looked outside. Everything looked normal.

He saw just what he expected to see: a fresh blanket of snow covering a pleasant, tidy neighborhood in Grand Rapids, Michigan, 1955. The street was completely quiet, the houses were dark. On the front lawn, a snowman stood guard in the lightly falling snow.

He heard a sound from the hallway and turned. It was the sleigh bell again! Moving to the door, he silently opened it and tiptoed out.

From the top of the hall stairs, he surveyed the empty living room. The stockings hung limply from the mantelpiece. There were no presents under the tree. A plate of cookies and a glass of milk sat untouched on the coffee table.

Suddenly, the jingling sound returned. This time it was coming from the kitchen! The Boy leaned over the railing to get a better look. His eyes widened as he caught sight of a shadow on the dining room floor, the bright kitchen light making it all the darker. It looked like the shadow of a chubby little man carrying a sack on his back. As he waddled toward the Boy, a sleigh bell jingled with his every step.

This was it! Santa!

But then the shadow split in two, becoming the separate shapes of a thin man and a small girl.

The Boy's face fell. It was just his father and his sister.

"All right, Sarah, you've had your water," said their father. "Back to bed."

The Boy sprinted up the stairs and back into his room before they saw him and peeked through his keyhole as Sarah was tucked in across the hallway. Through her open door, he could see his father's back, but not his face.

". . . but he said Santa would have to fly faster than the speed of light to make it to every house in one night," Sarah was saying worriedly. "And to hold everyone's presents his sled would have to be bigger than an ocean liner. And . . ."

The Boy gulped. Through his keyhole he could see Sarah nod. There was a grave expression on her face. "He said he wasn't sure," she responded. "He wasn't sure Santa was for real."

"Of course Santa's real," her father assured her, smoothing her covers. "He's as real as Christmas itself." As if on cue, the sleigh bell jingled again, but now its source was all too apparent. Tucked into the back pocket of his father's pants was a Santa hat with a jingle bell sewn at the top.

Now their mother joined them. She was pregnant and had to lean back as she walked. "But he won't come until you're sound asleep," she said to Sarah, bending down to give her a kiss. "Sweet dreams."

"Santa will be here before you know it," Father added.

The Boy, watching his parents walk down the hall toward their room, was not so sure. The bell in his father's pocket jingled merrily.

The Boy grabbed a flashlight, opened his dresser drawer, and felt around until he found a small stack of framed black-and-white photos. There was one of him from three years ago, taken at Herpolsheimer's Department Store. He and his sister were happily sitting on the lap of Santa, who wore thick, heavy-framed glasses. His sister was pulling down Santa's fake beard.

Next, he pulled out a yellowed newspaper clipping. Its headline read, "Santas on Strike," and the photo showed a rowdy group of Santas, shaking their fists at the camera.

And finally, he took out of the drawer a copy of the *Saturday Evening Post*. On its cover was a painting by Norman Rockwell. It showed a small boy, pulling from a bottom drawer a Santa beard and coat. "The Discovery" was the cover line.

The hall light came on. The Boy doused the

flashlight and scrambled into bed as his door squeaked open. Tiptoeing into his room, his parents came to stand over him. The Boy was curled up with his back toward them, but he could see them reflected in an old Ford hubcap that was leaning against his radiator.

"He's dead to the world," his father whispered. "An express train couldn't wake him up."

"He used to try to stay up all night waiting for Santa," said his mother softly.

"I have a feeling those days are over."

"It would be sad if they were," she said.

"The end of the magic," murmured his father.

One of the Boy's eyes popped open. *What? The end of the magic? What magic?*

His mother bent down and gave him a gentle kiss. "Merry Christmas, sweetheart," she whispered.

Looking into the hubcap, the Boy watched his parents leave his room.

He rolled over, thinking. The wind-up clock on the bedside table ticked loudly. He checked the time — 10:21. Out the window, snow was falling.

He turned back and stared up at the model airplane that hung from the light fixture, a P-38 Lightning. The clock continued ticking. The Boy yawned, his eyelids getting heavy. His eyes began to close. As he drifted off, his father's words echoed in his head: *the end of the magic . . . end . . . of . . . magic.*

Some time later, something pierced his consciousness. Then he heard the ring of a sleigh bell. It was not, however, the thin, tinny sound of the bell on his father's cap. No, this bell had a full, rich, joyful jingle. This was a wonderful sound. The Boy's eyes popped open.

His clock said 11:55.

The bell continued jingling, louder and louder. Against the radiator, the hubcap vibrated faster and faster, and the P-38 started dancing madly on its wire. And then the entire room began to rumble. The radiator hissed, but the hissing sound was soon drowned out by something much louder: a full-blown, ear-piercing steam whistle.

Flash! Flash! Flash! A blinding light pulsed through the window as a deafening roar thundered from down the street. The Boy jumped up on all fours on his bed to look out the window.

A huge, boiling cloud of steam hung in the center of the street. Behind the steam cloud flickered strange yellow squares of light, like windows flashing past. As he watched, the flickering squares began to slow. He heard the sound of crunching and grinding metal.

A cloud of steam billowed up to the window,

obliterating the Boy's view of the street. He dove off his bed, jumped into his slippers, and pulled his robe off the bedpost. *Rrriiippp!* The pocket of his robe tore open, sending a couple of marbles rattling to the floor.

Pounding down the stairs, he flung open the front door, ran up the snow-covered path, and skidded to a stop.

Wow!

The cloud of steam in the middle of the street began to evaporate, slowly revealing . . . a train. But what a train! It was a full-sized passenger train, and it had stopped just a few feet from his front lawn. A glistening, black beauty, a classic old-time steam locomotive, it was coupled to a huge open coal car and a train of passenger cars that stretched the length of a football field. The coaches sparkled, their windows glowing brightly. The engine creaked and hissed as the train waited.

Mesmerized, the Boy approached the train. The cars seemed to loom about ten stories tall. Smoke rose from the locomotive's huge stack, and the headlight cast an eerie yellow glow on the falling snow.

The Boy stared in awe for a long moment and then glanced up the street. Every house on the block was dark and quiet. Not a neighbor stirred.

Behind the Boy, a conductor, wearing a uniform complete with pillbox cap and shiny brass buttons on his vest, stepped down the three stairs from the passenger car. He pulled an oversized pocket watch out of his vest and checked it. "All aboard!" he shouted emphatically.

The Boy spun around, confused. Did the conductor mean him?

"All aboard!" the Conductor repeated. His face was hidden by a plume of steam rising from beneath the wheels of the passenger car. "Well? You coming?"

"Where?" asked the Boy.

The Conductor leaned through the steam, and the Boy finally got a good look at him. He was a pleasant-looking man with wire-rimmed eyeglasses and a mustache. He also had, the Boy noticed, a strangely contradictory quality about him; his sparkling eyes promised either thrills and adventure or danger and terror. Or both. It was hard to tell.

The Conductor put his watch away. "Ah, a young man in need of answers," he said, giving the Boy a knowing look. "Why, the North Pole, of course. *This* is the Polar Express."

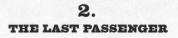

SURE enough, there it was, spelled out in large gold letters on the side of the gleaming passenger car: *The Polar Express*. He looked back at the Conductor. "North Pole?" he said hesitantly.

Over the top of his spectacles, the Conductor gave the Boy a hard look. "I see," he said. "Hold this, please."

Handing the Boy his lantern, he produced a clipboard. "Is this you?" he asked, pointing to a name on the list. The Boy nodded. "It says here . . ." the Conductor continued, reading, ". . . no Santa photo from the department store this year . . . no letter to Santa . . . your sister had to put the milk and cookies out by herself." He shook his head gravely. "It seems this is your crucial year. If I were you, I'd think about getting on board." He gave the Boy a knowing wink and took back the lantern. "I'm on a schedule, ya know."

Still unsure, the Boy stepped back, away from the train.

"Suit yourself," the Conductor said curtly. He signaled to the engineer, and the engine sounded two short blasts of the whistle. There was a burst of steam, and the Conductor disappeared into the car.

The Boy stood there. The train shuddered and jerked, and began to creep forward. And just like that, the Boy made his decision. He climbed aboard.

From the platform between the cars, the Boy looked back. The front lawn, his house, his parents, his sister — his whole life — were receding into the distance.

The Conductor appeared beside the Boy on the platform and opened the coach door for him, giving him that same knowing smile. "Welcome aboard," he said.

The passenger car was filled with a many very happy children, an even mix of boys and girls who ranged in age from about five to nine. They all wore pajamas or nightgowns.

As he walked down the aisle, the Boy felt nervous. When he found an empty seat, he checked out his fellow travelers. They all seemed full of expectation and excitement. Sitting behind him, across the aisle, was a pretty, pleasant-looking girl, who — *Yikes!* — smiled at him! The Boy immediately averted his eyes, staring at his slippers.

"Hey!" yelled a voice. A kid was leaning over the seat in front of the Boy. "Yeah, you," said the kid.

The Boy looked up.

In truth, the kid looked a little goofy. He wore thick Coke-bottle glasses and had a know-it-all attitude about him. As a matter of fact, that's what the Boy immediately decided to call him.

The Know-It-All leaned farther over his seat back, pushing his face a bit too close to the Boy. "You know what kind of train this is?" he demanded.

"Huh . . . ?"

"Train," repeated the boy. "Do you know what kind of train this is? Well, do ya?"

"Uh . . ." said the Boy.

"It's a magic train!" said the Girl. "We're going to the North Pole!"

The Know-It-All rolled his eyes. "Of course it's a magic train, but what *kind?*" Not waiting for an answer, he rushed on: "It's a Baldwin 2-8-4 S3-class Berkshire-type steam locomotive built in 1931 at the Baldwin locomotive works at Eddystone,

Pennsylvania, has a 69-inch driver wheel diameter with a 26-inch cylinder bore and a 34-inch stroke engine weighs 456,100 pounds has a tractive force of 83,450 pounds at 5,000 drawbar horsepower top speed is . . ."

With a sudden lurch, the train rumbled around a sharp curve. The Know-It-All immediately spun around to look out his window. "We're hanging a left on Monroe!" he yelled at the top of his lungs.

"He's kind of a know-it-all," the Girl whispered to the Boy, pointing her chin toward the offender.

"I guess," said the Boy. But he was thinking about something else. "Are we really going to the North Pole?" he asked her.

The Girl nodded enthusiastically. "Isn't that wonderful?" she said.

Before the Boy could respond, the Know-It-All broke in. "Herplosheimer's! Herplosheimer's!" he shouted.

A huge cheer erupted from the children. Some of them clearly recognized the name, and the others just followed their enthusiasm. The children ran to the Boy's side of the car and pressed their noses against the cold glass.

There it was, as big as life: Herplosheimer's Department Store, with its famous Christmas window. This year the theme was "The Night Before Christmas." The scene in the window depicted an old-fashioned living room. There was a fireplace with stockings and a Christmas tree with presents under it. A life-sized mechanical Santa filled the stockings and then turned with a pronounced jerk.

The kids oohed and aahed at the scene, and at the many beribboned toys that it displayed. They fogged the windows with their breath. The Know-It-All quickly wiped a spot clear and pointed at the toys. "Look at all those presents. I want 'em all!"

The Girl, meanwhile, was staring at the angel on top of the tree. "It's all so . . . beautiful," she murmured.

The Boy looked too, but what he saw was something altogether different: the clockwork Santa, its mechanical skeleton sticking out through its coat. A stream of hydraulic fluid ran down Santa's pant leg, collecting in a puddle on the floor. The Boy shook his head. What an obvious fake.

"Tickets," called a voice behind him. "Tickets, please." All business, the Conductor stopped beside the Boy's seat. He looked down. "Ticket?" he said to the Boy.

The Boy sat frozen. "What ticket?" he choked out.

"Let's not dilly-dally. I'm on a schedule, ya know." The Conductor pointed to the Boy's robe. "Pocket?" he said helpfully.

The Boy reached into his robe. His hand passed through the huge hole that had ripped when he'd grabbed the robe.

"The other one?" suggested the Conductor.

The Boy checked his other pocket. To his astonishment, he found a long, gold-colored ticket. Engraved in fancy script, it read, *One Round Trip — North Pole.*

Amazed, the Boy handed it over, whereupon, with a flourish, the Conductor pulled a gleaming, silver ticket punch out of his vest and began punching.

CLICK . . . CLICK, CLICK . . . CLICK, CLICK, CLICK, CLICK CLICK, CLICK, CLICK, CLICK, CLICK, CLICK . . . The Conductor punched dozens of holes into the ticket, creating a blizzard of tiny paper cutouts. He held it up to check his handiwork, then handed the ticket back to the Boy.

Suddenly the Conductor noticed a boy playing with the emergency brake. "Young man!" he barked to the boy, who was missing his front teeth. "Climb down from there! That's not a toy." He moved off to deal with the situation.

Meanwhile, the Boy looked down at his

punched ticket, and noticed something very strange indeed. Letters. The holes formed letters. The first letter was a B, the last one was an E. And in between were some spaces. It was weird.

The Boy gave the Girl a confused look, and she just shrugged. But the Know-It-All, naturally, had something to say about it. He leaned over his seat. "That guy sure likes to show off with his hole puncher," he said, whipping out his own ticket. "Look what that wise guy punched on mine."

The Boy looked down at the Know-It-All's ticket. It had an L and an E punched next to each other, with spaces after the E.

"L, E . . . what's that supposed to mean?" the Know-It-All demanded.

The Boy and the Girl had no idea, but the Know-It-All was already on to something else. He turned to the window, suddenly suspicious. "Hey! Wait a minute. Just a minute. We're headed to"— he paused for dramatic effect — *the other side of the tracks!"*

All the children turned to look out the windows. The train passed a cemetery, and beyond it, the houses were smaller and worn down. There was very little Christmas cheer here. As the Polar Express rumbled by, dogs growled at it. As if in response, the train's brakes began to groan.

The Conductor picked up a microphone that was hanging by the door. "Edbrooke Avenue," he announced. "Next stop, 11344 Edbrooke Avenue."

The train shuddered to a halt in front of the saddest, loneliest, most depressing house on the block, the very last one. The air brakes hissed loudly.

The Know-It-All slid his window down and stuck his head out for a look. Shoving his ticket into his pocket, the Boy lowered his window and poked out his head as well.

Standing by the bottom step of the passenger car was another boy. He stood with his head hanging down, looking very lonely.

The Conductor stepped off the train, and there followed a repetition of the earlier exchange between the Conductor and the Boy.

"Well?" the Conductor asked the Lonely Boy. "You coming?"

"Just another pickup," said the Know-It-All, yawning to show how unimpressed he was. He shut his window and plopped back into his seat.

But the Boy continued to watch.

"Why, the North Pole, of course," the Conductor was now saying to the new fare. "*This* is the Polar Express."

The Lonely Boy did not move, as the Conductor checked his clipboard. "I've got a schedule, ya know," said the Conductor in exactly the same tone he'd used with the Boy.

The Conductor signaled the engine with his lantern and climbed on board as the whistle blew two short blasts. But this time it was different. The Lonely Boy was still not moving, or even looking up. He wasn't coming.

The Conductor looked out at him one last time as the pistons slowly began to turn the driver wheels, the big wheels that powered each car. The cars lurched forward as the slack was pulled from the couplers. The train began to pick up speed.

The Boy watched as the Lonely Boy was left behind. But then, at the last second, the Lonely Boy looked up. Had he changed his mind? Yes! He started after the train, but now it was moving faster.

"Hey!" the Boy shouted. "The kid wants to get on the train!" But no one did anything. Now the Lonely Boy was right beside the Boy's window. He looked directly at the Boy, and a connection was established between them. *Help me,* said the look on the Lonely Boy's face.

"Come on. Run!" shouted the Boy out the window.

And the Lonely Boy ran! Faster and faster, gaining on the train, as close to the edge of the tracks as he could. He reached for a handhold. He almost had it! One more inch! But then he slipped in the snow, losing precious ground. The train pulled away from him. He wasn't going to make it.

The Boy pulled his head into the car and shouted: "We've got to stop the train!"

The kids froze. They had no idea what was going on. Frantic, the Boy looked around.

"There!" cried the Girl, pointing at the cord for the emergency brake. The Boy grabbed it and pulled it hard.

Skkrrreeeeee! The brakes locked up, all the kids tumbled forward, and the Polar Express shuddered to a stop.

The Boy picked himself up off the floor. Outside, the Lonely Boy sprinted to catch up with the train, managing to clamber on board just as the train started to move again. From the vestibule, he looked through the porthole window and his eyes met the Boy's for a moment. He then turned and entered the empty, rear observation car.

"All right," said the fearsome voice behind the Boy. "Who pulled that cord?" The Conductor! The Boy gulped.

3.
RUNAWAY TICKET

THE Conductor stood in the doorway, hands on hips. He wanted an answer, and he wanted it now.

"He did," said the Know-It-All, pointing a finger at the Boy.

The Boy couldn't believe it. What a rat.
"In case you didn't know," said the Conductor, "that cord is for emergency use only. And in case you aren't aware, tonight is Christmas Eve. And if you haven't noticed, this train is on a very tight schedule. Now, young man, Christmas may not be important to *some* people" — here he cast a significant look at the Boy — "but it is *very* important to most of us."

"I just —" the Boy began to protest.

"All he did was stop the train so that kid could get on," the Girl interrupted. She pointed back toward the observation car, and the Conductor took a look. Through the window he could see the Lonely Boy taking a seat in the observation car. He was the only one in the car.

The Conductor turned to the Boy. "Is that what happened, young man?"

The Boy nodded.

The Conductor's tone softened. "Well, let me remind you that we are on a schedule," he admonished, "and . . ."

The lecture petered out. The Conductor pulled out his oversized pocket watch. Snapping open the lid, he looked at the watch and gulped audibly. Now the Boy started to worry, seeing the worried look on the Conductor's face.

The Conductor snapped his watch shut and tucked it back into his vest pocket. "I've never been late before," he said decisively. "I'm certainly not going to be late this year. So no more emergency stops." He looked as severe as possible.

The whistle blasted.

"Now," said the Conductor more cheerfully. "Are there any Polar Express passengers in need of refreshment?"

Every arm in the car reached for the stars.

"That's what I thought," said the Conductor. "Everyone take your seats, please."

The kids ran to their seats, the Conductor slid the door open, and . . . BLAM! A dozen singing, dancing, roller-skating waiters bounded into the car to serve hot chocolate. They wore white uniforms with aprons, and bow ties, and they all had matching mustaches. Maybe they were Swiss, or maybe Italian. It was hard to say. But at any rate, they were jaunty and friendly, and they sang with great gusto, a song about hot chocolate. They tap-danced, skated, slid, flipped, and twisted. They juggled as they tossed cups, spoons, and saucers to the thirsty kids. The Conductor joined in, singing and dancing along.

As soon as the kids were done drinking, the waiters scooped up the dirty cups and saucers. And, *zip!* they were gone. All that remained was a chocolate mustache on each amazed child.

The Know-It-All was spouting, but no one was listening. "Montezuma, king of the Aztecs, would drink fifty quarts of hot chocolate every day," he said. "It was as thick as mud and red, because he put chili peppers in it instead of sugar. Get it? *Hot* chocolate."

The Girl reached under her seat and came up with a cup of hot chocolate topped with a huge mound of whipped cream. "For him," she said, nodding toward the Lonely Boy. "I'm going to take it to him."

"Aren't we supposed to stay in our seats?" said the Boy. He was worried now about the Conductor's wrath.

Doubt shadowed her face, but she still got up.

"Yeah," the Know-It-All chimed in. "It's a violation of railroad safety regulations for a kid to cross between moving cars without a grownup! Everybody knows that."

"I think it'll be okay," said the Girl. She headed toward the door.

The Boy watched through the window as the Girl handed the Lonely Boy his hot chocolate and the Conductor punched his ticket with a few quick strokes. It was not at all the extravagant procedure that the Conductor had used to punch the Boy's ticket.

"Did you see that?" said the Know-It-All to the others. "He hardly punched *anything* on that kid's ticket."

Glancing down, the Boy spotted a ticket, just sitting there on the Girl's seat. It hadn't been punched at all. The Boy picked it up and headed to the coach door.

"Hey! What're you doing?" the Know-It-All demanded. "You're going to get us all in trouble!"

Ignoring him, the Boy pulled the door open and stepped out. The wind blew ferociously, and the roar of the train was deafening. The platform was covered in ice and snow, and the space between the cars seemed to be twenty feet wide. The two cars rocked violently out of rhythm with each other. Staring down at the grinding couplers, the Boy saw the track rushing by in a blur, and heard the wheels screaming. The Boy hesitated, took a deep breath, closed his eyes, and . . .

Slam!

The door, swinging behind him, hit his rear end, nearly knocking him off his feet. He grabbed hold of an iron handhold and broke his fall . . . *but he dropped the ticket!*

As the ticket spiraled wildly in the wind, the Boy grabbed frantically for it, but he just couldn't reach it. It sailed above the train, seeming to take on a life of its own. As the wind gusted higher and higher, the ticket soared above the treetops and he lost sight of it.

The Polar Express kept rolling, and the light from the passenger car windows flickered through the trees outside. On its own journey now, the ticket flew into a cold, dark forest: the Great North Woods. The snow had stopped, and the sky was clear and full of stars. The wind died down, and moonlight glinted off the ticket's gold ink as it floated gently toward the ground.

Whoosh! A great gray blur flashed by: a pack of wolves, running through the trees. The air current they created lofted the ticket upward. It flapped hard, trying to catch up to the train as it crossed a bridge in the distance.

But the ticket was not to reach its destination, for now an eagle snatched it from the air in mid-flight. The bird went into a steep dive down a waterfall, and delivered the ticket to a hungry baby eaglet that was perched in a nest atop a tower of stone in the center of the river. *Ptoo!* The eaglet spat it out.

Now the ticket formed itself into a soaring paper airplane, flying down another waterfall and shooting through the forest, still looking for the train. Turning in the direction of the whistle, it smacked right into a tree, tumbling down into the snow. It rolled down a hill, gathering speed and snow until it had become a tiny snowball. Then it fell off a ledge and hit a stone, which broke apart the snow.

Free again, the ticket floated parachute-like into a dark space. It was a tunnel — the train tunnel. And at that very moment, the train was barreling through it. The train's light caught the ticket just before it smacked into the cowcatcher and held on for dear life. But the wind that whirled around the train was too much for the ticket, and it lost its fragile grip, skipping and spiraling toward the rear of the train. Then, *smack:* it slapped up against the sole of a shoe. It was a size 13, with a hole in it larger than a silver dollar.

After a moment, a gust of wind sent the ticket flying again, past the reclining body of a very large man. He was clad in dirty trousers, a tattered jacket, a frayed shirt, and grimy red gloves whose fingers had long since worn away.

4.
THE KING OF THE NORTH POLE

T

HE man was a hobo. In classic hobo fashion, he had made his bed in a burlap hammock that hung beneath one of the train's cars. He had a large, gentle face, and he was sound asleep, snoring loudly. His tweed cap was pulled down over his eyes, and he used his "bindle," a bundle of his belongings tied into a red kerchief, for a pillow. The ticket plastered itself onto the hobo's cheek. It tickled. He swatted it off, and it was airborne once again.

It flew upward between two of the cars and past the platform, where the Conductor and the Girl were crossing back between the cars. The ticket hovered behind the Conductor as the Girl opened the coach door. Once the door was open, the draft sucked the ticket into the passenger car, the very same one in which it had started out. No one noticed it.

As the Conductor continued down the aisle, the Girl took the seat beside the Boy. He looked up at the Girl, about to confess that he'd lost her ticket, but before he could do it, the Conductor was back.

The Girl looked up at the Conductor, who loomed above her, checking his clipboard.

"You got on in . . . Chicago," he said, looking down the list. "I don't believe I punched your ticket."

Having no pockets in her nightgown, the Girl checked her seat. No ticket.

"I left it right here on the seat, but it's gone," she said helplessly.

"Are you saying . . . you've *lost your ticket?*" he thundered.

A hush fell over the passenger car. All eyes were focused on the unfolding drama. The Girl nodded meekly.

The Conductor gave her a "we've got a problem" look.

"She didn't lose her ticket," the Boy said. "I did."

Now all eyes turned in his direction, but he was looking at the Girl. "I went to bring it to you, but the wind blew it out of my hand . . ." he began. He looked down at his slippers. "I'm sorry."

The Conductor looked down at the girl. "I'll need you to come with me, young lady," he said.

He took the Girl by the arm and led her solemnly toward the rear door. It closed behind them.

For a moment there was stunned silence in the car. Then the Know-It-All jumped to his feet. "You know what's gonna happen to her, don'tcha? He's gonna throw her off the train," he announced excitedly.

The children gasped, and the Boy's eyes widened in horror. He ran to the rear-door window, in time to see the Conductor leading the Girl toward the back of the observation car. It looked as if she was in big trouble. They passed the Lonely Boy, who kept his head down but shot a sideways glance toward the Girl.

The Know-It-All slithered up behind the Boy. "Yep," he said, "he'll probably throw her off the rear platform."

The Conductor escorted the Girl out onto the rear platform, closing the door behind him.

The Boy began frantically pacing the aisle. What to do?

At his ear, the Know-It-All would not shut up. "That's standard procedure," he explained confidently. "That way she won't get sucked under the wheels. Sometimes they slow the train down, but they never stop it."

The Boy ceased pacing. He'd been given the solution! "We have to stop the train!" he shouted.

The Know-It-All gasped, along with all the others. "No!" they yelled. "You can't! Not again!" But the Boy was already in motion. He jumped up onto the nearest seat and reached for the emergency pull-cord.

But then something caught his eye. It was a long yellow rectangle, pressed across the grate of an air intake vent. *The ticket.* The Boy froze. He blinked a few times, completely stunned. Then he reached out and grabbed the ticket off the grate. Squeezing it tightly, he sprinted out onto the icy platform, stuck the ticket between his teeth, grabbed the railing, and leaped across. He landed on the other side, wrenched open the door, and dashed through the observation car. The Lonely Boy didn't even look up.

At the rear door of the car, the Boy swung the door open.

Nothing. No one was there — only the frozen mountains and the moonlit rails receding into the distance.

The Boy ran back to the Lonely Boy. "Where'd they go?" he said wildly.

The Lonely Boy shrugged and fiddled with his ticket.

"What happened to them?" the Boy persisted.

Another shrug.

"Look, she's in trouble. Help me," he pleaded.

The Lonely Boy looked up and slowly pointed his finger toward the ceiling. Glancing out the window, the Boy saw two shadows, the shadows of the Girl and the Conductor, playing on the cliffs outside. They were on the roof! The Boy ran for the door.

On the rear deck, he spotted a ladder on the side of the car which bore fresh footprints on its snow-covered rungs. The Boy stuck the ticket back between his teeth and began climbing. The snow had begun again, coming down hard.

When he reached the lip of the roof, he caught a fleeting glimpse of the Girl and the Conductor trudging along the coach roof, but they vanished behind the curtain of thick falling snow. The lantern's flame was all the Boy could see. Then it disappeared.

The Boy cautiously shimmied up onto the roof. He slowly stood and gained his balance, still clutching the ticket. The wind and snow lashed his hair as the spectacular wilderness rushed by. Smoke from the engine billowed overhead.

Now the Boy spotted two sets of footprints in

the snow. One set was large, the other small. Walking with extreme care, the Boy followed them, inching forward along the roof. The snow squall was so thick that the Boy could barely see. Faintly, he could hear a strange, metallic melody from up ahead, accompanied by a gravelly humming.

Then the Boy saw an amber glow. He walked closer and found that it was not the lantern that was glowing — it was a campfire. A campfire burning in the middle of the observation car roof.

Sitting on an orange crate by the fire was a hobo. A pot of coffee brewed over the fire, a pair of wet socks dangled over the pot. He wore grimy red gloves with the fingers worn away. The Hobo stopped cranking his hurdy-gurdy, which was the source of the music.

"Well, lookie what we have here," he said.

The Boy had never seen a hobo before, not to mention a campfire on top of a train.

"What can I do for you?" the Hobo asked cheerfully.

"Ah . . . I'm looking for this girl."

A big smile spread across the Hobo's face. "Ain't we all," he said with a big belly laugh. "Ain't we all."

"I've got her ticket," the Boy explained.

The Hobo took the ticket and held it up to the

moonlight. "Well, whaddaya know? A genuine, authentic, official ticket to ride the Polar Express." He handed the ticket back to the Boy. "I'd put that in a safe place, I was you. I keep all my valuables right here, in my size thirteens." He tapped one of his huge shoes.

Following the advice, the Boy stashed the ticket in his slipper. Meanwhile, the Hobo wrung out his socks and began putting them on. "'Course, I don't use 'em myself," he said. "Tickets. I ride for free. I ride this rattler whenever I feels like it."

He launched into what even the Boy could tell must have been a classic hobo boast. "This here's my train. I'm the king of this train. King of the Pol Ex. King of the North Pole." He stopped briefly. "Where's my manners? Sit down. Take a load off! Have a cup of joe!" He offered the Boy some foul-smelling coffee, but the Boy shook his head.

"What about Santa?" he asked, sitting down beside the Hobo. "Isn't he the King of the North Pole?"

The Hobo roared with laughter. "Santa? Ha! Ha! Ha! That's rich! What *about* Santa? Ha! Ha! Ha! . . . Ho! Ho! Ho!" Then the King pulled a cheap Santa hat out of his back pocket, very similar to the one the Boy's father had had, but this one was worn and tattered. It had a single sleigh bell sewn on top. He rang the bell and put the cap on, ho-ho-ho-ing like Santa. Then he stopped abruptly, fixing the Boy with a suspicious look. "Exactly what is your persuasion? When it comes to the Big Man . . . if you don't mind me asking?"

The Boy took a moment to gather his thoughts. "Well, I want to believe, but —"

The King cut him off. "But!" he mocked. He doused the fire with what was left of the coffee, stuffed the pot and the rest of his belongings miraculously into his bindle, and turned to the Boy. "You don't want to be bamboozled," he said, "led down the garden path . . . duped . . . conned . . . have the wool pulled over your eyes . . . hoodwinked . . . taken for a ride . . ." The King paused, smiling that sly smile of his. "Railroaded, so to speak."

The King threw his sack over his shoulder. "Let's go find that dame," he said, and trudged through the heavy snow toward the engine. The Boy followed. The blizzard was so severe that the Boy lost sight of the King for a moment, but then he reappeared. "Oh, one thing," the King shouted back at the Boy. "Do you believe in ghosts?"

The Boy shook his head.

The King smiled that sly smile again. And then, suddenly, he really did disappear, right into the whiteout.

5.
JUMP!

HELLO?" called the Boy. He couldn't see anything at all, only the raging blizzard. Very afraid now and all alone, the Boy turned and slowly headed back to the rear of the train. The snow was getting deeper by the second, piling up above the Boy's ankles. When he reached the end of the car, the gap between the cars seemed wider now, ridiculously dangerous. There was no way he could jump it. He turned back toward the front of the train. The snow was now up to his waist.

The Boy was so exhausted, he could barely wade through the heavy snow. He fell to his knees. "Help," he said weakly.

The snow came up to his neck.

"Help!"

What on earth had he gotten himself into?

"Help," he whispered.

The whistle blew, startling the Boy. All he saw was snow. The whistle blew again, and he began to be aware of a voice, mixed in with the shriek of the whistle. "Helllooooo," it called.

The boy straightened up, unsure of what he'd heard. In a moment, he saw a beam of light, waving through the falling snow like a flashlight. It was moving toward him along the top of the train.

"Over here!" he shouted.

The light beam moved closer. Then, materializing out of the snow, was the King. A battery-powered headlamp was strapped to his forehead. He had a ski pole in each hand, and a pair of old-fashioned cross-country skis tied to his boots.

"Quick," said the big fellow, "git up on my shoulders. We ain't got much time." He crouched as low as he could and began to haul the worn-out Boy out of the snow. "Hurry up, get on. It's the only way we'll make it in time."

The urgency in the King's voice finally got the Boy's attention. He climbed up onto the King's huge shoulders, straddling his neck, hanging on to his chin. The King began wading through the snow toward the front of the train.

"We have to get to the engine 'fore we reach Flat Top Tunnel," said the King.

"Why's that?"

The Polar Express was now slowly climbing a slight grade.

"'Cause they's only a one-inch clearance between the top of this here train and Flat Top Tunnel," the King told him.

The snow squall stopped, and suddenly the Boy could see. Uh-oh. *"Looook!"* he screamed. There, at the bottom of the steep hill they were about to descend, was Flat Top Tunnel. It looked like a little tiny mouse hole.

The locomotive started dropping down the steep hill, with the coal tender and then the other cars following it. Atop the train, the King went into a ski crouch. He tucked his poles under his arms and pushed off. "Hold on!" he yelled. The Boy, riding high on the King's shoulders, had a perfect view of the disaster coming at him. Flat Top Tunnel was now just ahead, looking to the Boy like a huge, fiendish face.

Carrying the Boy, the King jumped the gap between cars and landed hard. One more car to go. The Boy was terrified.

"There's only one trick to this, kid," said the King. "When I say jump . . . you . . . JUMP!"

The engine blasted into the tunnel's mouth.

Slap: the duo jumped the last gap. The coal tender, a low, open car, was just ahead.

The Boy looked up and saw the tunnel-top shearing straight toward him. Sparks were now flying as the tunnel mouth shaved the snow and an inch of metal from the top of the engine.

The King shouted at the top of his lungs, "...*Jump!*"

The Boy jumped.

He dove through the thin space between the tunnel entrance and the coal tender, into total blackness.

It stayed dark for a long time. Only the roar and rattle of the train could be heard.

And then they were out of the tunnel, and the Boy found himself lying in a bed of coal.

Suddenly, with the loud grinding sound of metal on metal, the coal beneath the Boy dropped away and the Boy tumbled down a chute, landing with a thump on the floor of the locomotive cab. A load of coal poured down behind him.

The Boy took a look around. There was no sign of the King anywhere. He had fallen into a wilderness of pipes, valves, levers, and gauges. A fire blazed in the firebox. And sitting on the engineer's bench was the Girl. She wore a striped engineer's hat that covered her whole head and huge gloves that reached up to her armpits. She rested her arm casually on the sill of the open window, her hand on the throttle, and gave the Boy a big smile.

The Boy scrambled to his feet. "But I thought you were thrown —" he began, bewildered. "You're — driving the train?"

"They put me in charge," she said. "They had to go check the headlamp. Isn't it great?"

The Boy scrutinized the controls, fascinated. "But how do you . . . do you know how?"

"It's easy," she replied cheerily. "Here, I'll show you." She began pointing out levers and gauges. "This big lever here is the throttle. This little one is the brake. These are the pressure gauges . . . and this rope is the whistle." She pointed to the thick hemp cord hanging above her head.

"Whistle?" he said, his eyes lighting up.

"Wanna try it?"

Did he ever. He grabbed hold of the cord and gave it a good hard tug, producing a long blast from the whistle. The Boy pulled it again. It was glorious. "I wanted to do that my whole life!" he shouted.

THE sound of the whistle mixed with another sound, which the Boy could not immediately place. *Ooooooooww!* it went. It seemed to be coming from outside. The Boy stuck his head out the window to look, and there, on the roof, were two very bizarre-looking men. They were trying to change the bulb in the headlamp at the front of the engine.

"Steamer the Engineer and Smokey the Fireman," the Girl whispered to the Boy.

Steamer was short and fat. He weighed 444 pounds and stood 4 feet, 4 inches. He was bald, with a jowly cherubic face and a lazy left eye.

At 6 feet, 6 inches, Smokey stood constantly bent over. He weighed 66 pounds, and looked as if he might blow away in the wind. Wild orange hair stuck out from beneath his cap. His long, red beard hung to his feet, its tip singed and smoking. His right eye was decidedly cockeyed.

The sound that the Boy had heard was issuing from the mouth of Smokey, who was howling like a banshee as Steamer used Smokey's beard to hoist all 444 of his pounds up to the lamp housing.

"Hold me there!" Steamer yelled in a thick hillbilly accent.

"Ow! My hair!" Smokey screamed in the same accent.

Steamer finally screwed the bulb into the socket, and it sparked to life. A bright white beam flared across the tracks. Steamer let go of Smokey's beard and dropped onto the platform atop the cowcatcher, which caused Smokey to ricochet upward and clang his head inside the bell. Smokey's head vibrated so hard that it became a blur.

Meanwhile, Steamer was looking ahead, down the now brightly lit track. His eyes bugged out in horror. "Stop the train!" he yelled at the top of his lungs.

Down the track, reflected in the pilot light beams, were two smaller points of light. Something was standing in the middle of the track!

As Steamer waved hysterically at the kids in

the cab, Smokey pulled his head out of the bell. His eyes popped at what he saw.

"Stop the train!" Steamer screamed again.

"Pull the brake!" Smokey yelled.

The Boy and the Girl finally reacted. The brake! Where was it? A dozen levers and valves stared back at them. The Girl reached for a small polished brass handle. "He told me this one's the brake," she said.

"Who told you?" the Boy asked.

"The engineer!"

"Steamer?"

"Who?"

"The engineer!" the Boy shouted.

"Yes!" she yelled back.

"What about this red one?" said the Boy, pointing to a big lever with a bright red handle. "This looks like a brake!"

The Girl grabbed the small brass lever. "This is the brake," she said.

"Are you sure?"

This question, as usual, caused the Girl to freeze. Once again she lost her confidence.

"Huh?" she said blankly.

"Are you *sure?*" the Boy repeated.

Paralyzed by indecision, the Girl panicked and slapped her hands to her face, covering her eyes.

Outside, the twins were not doing much better. The Polar Express thundered toward the two small dots of light, which blinked. They were definitely eyes.

Steamer covered his face, while Smokey covered his ears. "Stoooooppp . . . the . . . train!" Steamer yelled for the last, and loudest, time.

With only seconds to spare, the Boy let go of the red lever and pulled the brass handle. *Hissss!* The air brakes locked, all eight drivers ground to a halt, and the Boy and the Girl were thrown against the wall. It had worked!

Outside, Smokey was thrown off the pilot lamp and went tumbling onto Steamer. The train skidded down the rails until the cowcatcher stopped inches from the owner of the eyes, a four-hundred-pound bull caribou. He stood in the middle of the tracks, frozen in the headlight.

Behind him were thousands more — a breathtaking, majestic herd of Arctic caribou stretching for miles, nonchalantly crossing the tracks as Steamer and Smokey gaped.

The Conductor came rushing into the cab all in an uproar. "Why are we stop —" he began, but broke off when he spotted the Boy. "You! I should have known! Young man, are you bound and determined that this train *never* gets to the North Pole?"

Wordlessly, the Girl pointed out the window.

The Conductor had a look. "I see," he said, mostly to himself. "Caribou crossing. That's a fine kettle of fish. This will definitely put me behind schedule."

The Girl immediately followed the Conductor outside. "Come on!" she said to the Boy, motioning to him to come too.

Up front at the cowcatcher, the Conductor joined Steamer. Smokey sat up on the lamp housing.

"I reckon that herd's over a hundr'd thousand," Steamer said. "Maybe a million. It's gonna be hours 'fore them 'bou is done crossin' that track."

"A tough nut to crack," Smokey chimed in.

The Boy and Girl arrived and peered out at the immense herd spread across the tracks, while the Conductor stared down at his watch. He ran his finger inside his collar to get some air. "Yep . . . definitely in some serious jelly," he fretted.

"A real jam," Steamer agreed.

"A tight spot," said Smokey.

"Up a creek," said Steamer.

"Up a tree," Smokey opined.

"Lost in the grass," added Steamer.

At that moment, the Boy accidentally stepped on Smokey's dangling beard. "Ooooowwwuuuu-uuu!" Smokey hollered.

The caribou froze, and the entire herd turned toward the train as one.

The lead bull trumpeted back, answering Smokey: "Ooooowwwuuuuuuu!"

This gave the Conductor an idea. He grabbed Smokey' s beard and gave it two strong tugs. "Oowwwwuu! Oowwwwuuuu!" hollered Smokey.

The bull answered back. "Oowwwwuu! Oowwwwuuuu!"

The Conductor gave Smokey's beard three short tugs. "Owwwuu! Owwwuu! Owwwuu!" went Smokey.

And then the most amazing thing happened. In a moment of complete silence, the two hundred thousand head of caribou that were on the track . . . simply took three steps back. The track was clear.

"Now that's more like it," said the Conductor enthusiastically. "All ahead slow!" he yelled to Steamer.

Steamer and Smokey leaped into the cab through the window, and Smokey began shoveling like a madman. Steamer gave the whistle two short blasts, and then pushed the throttle a careful inch. He could not see, nor could anyone else, that the cotter pin on the throttle was slipping loose. This was a very bad thing.

The locomotive's driver wheels began to turn, ever so slightly, and the Polar Express began to move. Out on the cowcatcher, the Boy and Girl waved to the caribou as the engine rolled by. Like Jersey cows, the caribou looked blankly at the passing train. The Conductor checked his watch once more, still worried.

In the cab, Steamer gave the throttle another nudge. The train didn't speed up. Smokey, in the back stoking the firebox, gave Steamer a concerned look. Steamer gave the lever another shove, but the drivers just spun. Finally, he shoved the throttle full forward with all his might.

The cotter pin sheared off, and the throttle lever fell off its post.

"Jumpin' jeepers!" yelled Steamer as he tumbled to the floor. "The cotter pin sheared off!"

Outside the locomotive, a giant plume of smoke belched from the smokestack, and jets of steam shot out from between the wheels. The Polar Express lurched forward. Atop the cowcatcher, the Conductor, unaware of the problem in the cab, watched the last of the caribou pass by.

The train was climbing a hill, gaining speed as it went. "Tell the engineer to watch the speed," the Conductor said to the Girl, who was up on the roof.

"Watch the speed!" the Girl shouted down to the cab.

Meanwhile, Steamer and Smokey were crawling the cab on their hands and knees looking for the cotter pin. The engine roared.

"It's gotta be here somewheres!" Steamer yelled over the din.

"Huh?" Smokey replied helpfully.

"What?"

"What?"

The Polar Express continued to accelerate. Outside, the Conductor was becoming concerned about the train's increasing speed.

"We're going pretty fast," said the Boy worriedly.

"Tell the engineer to slow down," the Conductor again told the Girl.

The Girl called down to the cab. "Slow . . . down!" she yelled at the top of her lungs.

There was no response from the cab. No movement. Nothing.

The Girl strained to listen and was finally able to pick up, very faintly, shouting from the cab: "Huh? . . . what? . . . what . . . huh?"

"They can't hear me," the Girl told the Conductor.

"They can't?"

The Girl shook her head.

"Are you sure?"

The dreaded words. The Girl froze. "Hmm?" she said.

"Are you sure?" the Conductor repeated.

The Girl stood there, paralyzed.

"Are you sure they can't hear you?" the Conductor said again.

The Girl had completely lost her focus. "Ah . . . uh . . . uh . . ." she dithered.

"Why so tight-lipped?" the Conductor grilled her. "Clammed up? Buttoned down? Cat got your tongue?"

The roar of the train was deafening. The speed was really picking up, and it was hard for the three of them to keep their balance.

The Conductor furrowed his brows. "I don't like the look of this," he said. "Come on, young man." He turned to the tongue-tied Girl. "Let's go, gabby," he said. He turned and started toward the cab, when suddenly he caught sight of a sign whizzing by:

GLACIER GULCH:
REDUCE SPEED.

"Too late!" he cried. Pulling the terry cloth belt from the Boy's robe, he began lashing the Boy and the Girl to an iron handhold.

"Is everything all right?" fretted the Boy. "What should we do?"

"Well," the Conductor replied, "given the fact that we have no communication with the engineer . . . we're standing totally exposed on the front of the locomotive . . . the train seems to be accelerating uncontrollably . . . and we are rapidly approaching Glacier Gulch, which just happens to be the steepest downhill grade in the entire world . . . I suggest we all hold on — *tightly!*"

7.
ACROSS THE ICE

OUTSIDE, the Boy and Girl were now staring at the most terrifying vertical drop they had ever seen. The Polar Express plunged downward. The kids braced themselves as their stomachs dropped to their feet.

The train was now falling so steeply that inside the cab Smokey and Steamer found themselves in a zero-gravity environment, doing a slow-motion ballet. They kicked and breast-stroked through the air like a pair of crazy astronauts.

Suddenly, out of a pile of coal floated the pin, tumbling end over end in the weightlessness. Steamer paddled toward it and grabbed it.

"You got it!" Smokey screamed in Steamer's ear.

Startled, Steamer dropped the pin.

Now the train hit a dip and began roaring up an insanely steep grade, so steep that Steamer and Smokey instantly went from being weightless to weighing thousands of pounds. They slammed onto the floor like two tons of bricks, flattening like pancakes — until the train once again went into a steep drop. The Boy, the Girl, and the Conductor held on with all their might while, in the cab, Smokey and Steamer were airborne again. Smokey clanged off the cab ceiling, but Steamer got his head caught between two pipes and found himself dangling helplessly from the rafters.

The Polar Express screamed down the flimsy wooden trestle track, shaking and vibrating violently. As the Boy and Girl held on for dear life, a small smile appeared on the Conductor's face. He was enjoying this. He looked over at the Boy, whose eyes were screwed closed in terror. Then he looked at the Girl, who to her own amazement was wide-eyed, loving the ride.

Stretching out ahead of them was The Great Polar Ice Cap. Uh-oh.

The frozen Arctic Ocean lay there glistening in the moonlight. The tracks descended straight to the ice and then disappeared into the glassy, frozen ocean. This one was going to be a doozy. Even the Conductor braced for it.

"Hold on tight," he shouted to the kids. "The ice is frozen over the tracks!"

There was no stopping it. The engine hit the ice and its driver wheels spun uselessly, spitting crushed ice everywhere.

The Polar Express writhed on the ice like a snake, skating and skidding in wide serpentine arcs. With no friction beneath the wheels, the train picked up more and more speed. Pretty soon, the train had developed so much momentum that the rear observation car started to slide forward, catching up to the engine. The train was a giant semicircle sliding down the ice sideways.

"Look!" cried the Girl, pointing to the observation car, which was skidding up directly across from her. The Lonely Boy was still sitting inside. He stared blankly at the Girl, his expression weirdly calm in light of the terrifying slide of the train across the ice.

Quickly, Smokey shoved the cotter pin into the throttle, securing it to the post. He pulled it closed, then hit the brake.

The driver wheels immediately locked up, and the train skated wildly on the ice. On the cowcatcher, the Girl lost her grip and flew off the side of the engine. The Conductor grabbed her arm, but he slipped on the icy platform and went over the side as well.

Desperately, the Boy grabbed the Conductor's jacket with both hands. But the Conductor was just too heavy. The Boy strained, his slippers sliding all over on the ice of the platform. He was close to being pulled off with the others.

Suddenly, he was jerked upward. A huge red-gloved hand had him by his robe. With a mighty tug, the hand yanked all three people back onto the cowcatcher. They were safe!

Only the Boy saw the King. The big man winked at the Boy, putting his finger across his lips.

"Ssshhh," said the King.

Ppssssssssss, went a plume of steam. And the King vanished with the vapor. Poof.

Crash! One after another, the passenger car couplers pounded into one other. The cars pivoted on the engine, and the Polar Express slid backward. Then it slowly skidded to a stop. The engine hissed and creaked.

The Conductor and the Girl stood on the cowcatcher, catching their breath, and the Conductor gave the Boy a quick glance. "That was quite . . . remarkable, young man," he said. "Quick thinking on your part. I thought we were goners."

The Conductor untied his safety rope. "Now that's more like it," he said. "I'm going to find out what the dickens happened here." With that, he stepped onto the ladder that went up to the top of the locomotive and started climbing. The Boy and Girl followed.

From up on top, they could see the vastness of the frozen Arctic Ocean all around them. Skid marks carved into the ice recorded the train's wild path.

The Conductor walked over the top of the boiler toward the cab. Standing on the roof, the Conductor shouted down to the crew below. "What in the name of Mike —"

Crrraaaack!

Went the ice. Back where the train had first hit the frozen ocean, huge chunks of ice were now collapsing into the black water. *Crack! Crack! Crack!* Like falling dominoes, great chunks of ice were collapsing as the cracks raced toward the train.

"Let's get the blazes out of here!" the Conductor yelled.

Down in the cab, Steamer jammed the lever into full reverse. The driver wheels spun wildly, spraying huge showers of shaved ice into the air. The Polar Express highballed into reverse, snaking madly backward across the ice, away from the crack.

Crack! Crack! Crack! The collapsing ice was gaining on the train. The Conductor, the Boy, and the Girl watched helplessly from atop the cab.

"Faster!" urged the Conductor.

As the reversing train began to pull away from the advancing fissure, the rear cars fishtailed out of control. The train was about to jackknife!

Steamer pulled the throttle shut, the drivers locked up, and the Polar Express skidded insanely, heading back the way it had come. The engine whipped around in a sideways skid, and the train straightened out.

Steamer had the throttle pushed as far forward as it could go. Miraculously, the wheels dug into the ice, and the locomotive peeled out. The train sped forward across the frozen ocean, the crumbling ice fracture nipping at the rear wheels of the observation car.

The Boy leaned forward, pointing. "Look!" he cried.

"Tracks!" said the Conductor. "Dead ahead!"

There they were: the train tracks, sloping up out of the frozen water and connecting to a trestle on shore, just a mile ahead.

In the cab, Steamer was furiously manipulating the engine controls, sweat pouring off his bald dome. He kept the train on course by alternating the brake and throttle. Meanwhile, Smokey was shoveling coal into the firebox like a madman.

But they were not out of the woods yet, for now the crack in the ice caught up to the observation car and disappeared underneath.

Steamer threw a glance at the pressure gauge. "I'm losing pressure!" he yelled hysterically. "I need more steam! Smokey! *More steam!*"

Now the train was halfway to the tracks that would save them. But just then, up on top of the train, the Girl looked back. "Oh no!" she wailed.

Beneath the observation car, the ice was crumbling apart. The car was dangling by its coupler, its wheels helplessly bouncing on the ice floes.

It got worse. The jagged ice gash now raced under the train and out ahead of the engine. In a second it reached the track. The ice surrounding the train ruptured and cracked.

The Conductor dropped flat onto the roof of the cab. "Brace yourselves," he warned.

The Polar Express crashed through the ice. *But —*

It dropped only three feet, right onto the tracks in the water below. Ice and water gushed into the air. A giant steam cloud engulfed the locomotive as the freezing water hit the red-hot boiler.

The train blasted out of the water and up the trestle, screaming between the narrow walls of an ice canyon, speeding across the vast, barren tundra, and finally slamming through a switch and onto the main line.

The rhythm of the rails resumed a mellow tempo. The Boy and Girl shared a long look. What a ride!

8.
SANTA'S NEW CONCEPT

I wasn't afraid," said the Girl. "Were you?"

The Conductor turned to the Boy. "Young man," he said, "it's time for us to head back to our car. And you, miss," he added, turning back to the Girl, "you'd better get to shoveling coal. I'll come back for you once we arrive at the North Pole."

"But why does *she* have to stay here?" The Boy protested.

"She has to work for her passage," replied the Conductor.

"I don't have a ticket," the Girl explained.

"Yikes!" the Boy exclaimed. "I forgot! I found your ticket!"

The Boy pulled the Girl's ticket out of his slipper, and the Girl's face lit up like a Christmas tree. "Oh my goodness! Thank you!"

"Ahem," said the Conductor. "Well, in that case."

He pulled out his ticket punch. "Tickets . . . tickets, please," he said with relish. Then he went to town. Tiny paper circles fell like snow.

He handed the ticket back to the Girl.

The holes on her ticket formed an L and an E — just like Know-It-All's. The Girl and the Boy stared at it. What could that mean? The Girl tucked it inside the lacy front of her nightdress.

"All right, then, time for the *three* of us to head back," said the Conductor.

The Conductor and the two kids began scrambling across the top of the coal tender. Suddenly, the train jerked around a sharp curve, sending the Boy tumbling down a mound of coal. He just managed to get hold of a grab iron before he fell off the side.

"Whoa there," said the Conductor, helping him back into the tender.

The Boy dusted himself off and regained his shaky footing.

"Years ago," the Conductor recalled, "on my first Christmas Eve run, I was making my rounds up on the roof, and I slipped on the ice. I grabbed a

On Christmas Eve, the boy
is woken up by a loud
rumbling outside his window.

The Polar Express is waiting
outside in a cloud of steam.

The Conductor
asks the boy
if he is coming
to the North Pole.

The kids are in for
a ride of a lifetime!

The boy grabs
the elusive ticket.

Watch out for Flat Top!

A herd of caribou threatens
the Polar Express.

The Polar Express chugs
through the mountains,
nearing the North Pole.

The train enters North Pole City.
Elves are everywhere.

The kids are lost in
North Pole City!
Will they make it to the
gift ceremony in time?

Santa's zeppelin flies over
North Pole City, carrying gifts.

Santa gives the boy the
First Gift of Christmas.

The boy gets a special gift
on Christmas morning . . .

The bell rings for him,
    and for everyone who
truly believes.

hand iron and that broke loose. I slid and I fell."
Here he paused for dramatic effect.

"But I stayed on the train," he finished.

The Boy's eyes widened. The same thing had
happened to him! "Someone caught you?" he
asked.

The Conductor nodded as the snow swirled
around them. "Or some*thing*," he said porten-
tously.

The Girl looked at the Boy. *"The angel,"* she
whispered.

"Did you see him?" the Boy asked the Conductor eagerly. "What did he look like?"

The Conductor just smiled and climbed down
the short ladder to the next coach platform. The
Boy and the Girl followed.

"Sometimes," the Conductor said, "seeing is
believing. And sometimes"— he leaned closer to
make his point — "the most real things in the
world are the things we can't see."

Whoa. That was deep.

They reached a passenger car that the kids had
never entered before, and the Conductor pulled the
latch and slowly opened the door.

When their eyes finally adjusted inside the
dimly lit car, the kids' jaws dropped. The car was
filled with broken dolls. There were dolls of all

types: bride dolls, baby dolls, paper cutout dolls, teddy bears, and all kinds of un-stuffed animals. All of them were disheveled and disfigured. Thousands of them were crammed into the coach seats like so many orphans. The effect was extremely unsettling.

"The forsaken and the abandoned," the Conductor announced gravely.

The kids followed the Conductor down the aisle. Three bare lightbulbs hung from the ceiling, swaying with the motion of the train, creating wavering, eerie shadows.

Spotting a tattered and dirty teddy bear with one arm missing and its button eyes gone, the Girl gently lifted him. "It makes me want to cry, seeing toys treated this way," she said.

"And these are the lucky ones," the Conductor said.

"Why are they here?" asked the Boy.

"It's a new concept Santa came up with," the Conductor explained. "Instead of throwing them away, he collects them and the elves refurbish them. He calls it 're-bicycling', something like that."

The Girl set the bear down next to a half-charred bride doll, and a small tear fell from her eye.

At the far end of the car was a tangled rat's nest of marionettes, their strings a knotted, snarled mess. There were hundreds of them, hanging from the ceiling by their snarled control rods.

"The hopelessly tangled puppets," announced the Conductor. "The elves are the only ones who can untangle them. So we bring them back to Santa every Christmas Eve."

It was like a jungle. The Boy and Girl gazed in awe at string puppets of all shapes and sizes: clowns, pirates, fairies, kings, cowboys, Indians, witches, reptiles, and every type of animal.

"Come along quickly," the Conductor said. "We don't want to dilly-dally in *this* car." He took the Girl by the hand and they disappeared behind the maze of strings.

The Boy tried following them, but he had lost sight of them. He continued past the creepy puppets, pushing away their strings as if they were cobwebs. Most of the marionettes wore smiles, but they seemed forced, as if the dolls were in pain.

He passed a knight in armor, tangled up with a ballerina and curvy nightclub singer whose feather boa was wrapped around her spiked heels.

Finally, the Boy spotted the Conductor and the Girl at the car's rear door. The Conductor was rattling through his keys. "I can never find this one," he muttered.

The Conductor and the Girl didn't notice the Boy, as their backs were to him. The Boy took one more step and a hand landed on the Boy's shoulder with a thump. It was a gnarled hand, with long sharp fingernails. The Boy spun around and found himself face to face with a marionette that he recognized as Ebenezer Scrooge, the mean old man from *A Christmas Carol*. Jumping back, the boy instantly became tangled in the nightclub singer's strings. He was caught fast.

Completely unnerved, the Boy struggled helplessly against the strings.

"Ah, there we are," said a familiar voice. The Conductor, finding the right key, unlocked the door and pushed it open. A large gust of wind blasted in, and the marionettes swirled and bounced around.

Finally, with a tremendous effort, the Boy pulled himself free. He dashed to the Conductor and the Girl, and all three quickly escaped the car, slamming the door shut behind them.

PANTING hard, the Boy and the Girl leaned back against the door and looked around. They were back in the passenger car, and everything looked as it had before. The kids were all there, blissfully ignorant of all that was going on elsewhere on the train. The Conductor moved off to check someone's ticket.

Then, glancing into the observation car, the Boy noticed something disturbing. The car was empty. The Lonely Boy was gone, and the rear door of the car hung open, swinging in the wind.

The Girl also saw the empty observation car. She and the Boy headed toward the door.

"Hey, where are you going?" the Know-It-All called after them.

When the Boy and the Girl reached the icy platform outside, the Boy got ready to jump across the gap. "Careful," he said to himself as much as to her. "This can be tricky."

"Wait," said the Girl. She reached down, flapped a little hinged gangplank over the gap, and easily walked across. The Boy followed, astonished. Where had that come from?

As they entered the observation car, the Girl put her finger to her lips. "Listen," she whispered.

Now the Boy heard it too. It was the Lonely Boy, singing quietly to himself. It was beautiful, a melancholy Christmas ballad. The Girl and the Boy walked silently down the length of the car, listening.

I'm wishing on a star
And trying to believe
That even though it's far,
He'll find me Christmas Eve.

I guess that Santa's busy
'Cause he's never come around.
I think of him
When Christmas comes to town.

They found him standing at the railing of the rear platform, looking out to the night sky. How amazing the stars looked from this point on the earth! As the Lonely Boy sang, the swirling snow and sparking cinders passing overhead, together with the train's glowing red taillight, seemed to draw magical pictures in the air to illustrate what he was singing.

The Girl joined the song, but the Lonely Boy was not startled or self-conscious as his song became a duet.

The best time of the year:
When everyone comes home
With all this Christmas cheer,
It's hard to be alone.

Putting up the Christmas tree
With friends who come around,
It's so much fun
When Christmas comes to town.

Together, they represented both sides of Christmas: the Lonely Boy's singing was sad and haunting, the Girl's warm and joyous, and they alternated lines. The Boy just stood in the middle, listening.

When Santa's sleigh bells ring,
I listen all around.

The Herald Angels sing.
I never hear a sound.
And all the dreams of children,
Once lost will all be found.

They sang the last verse together:

That's all I want
When Christmas comes to town . . .
That's all I want
When Christmas comes to town.

After they shared a few minutes of silence, the Lonely Boy looked down at his slippers and spoke softly. "Thanks for stopping the train for me," he said.

The Boy nodded.

"Hey, you three," said a voice. It was the Conductor, emerging from the back door of the caboose. "We just crossed it," he called down. "Latitude sixty-six degrees thirty-three minutes. The Arctic Circle."

The children followed him back into the train. "Ladies and gentlemen," announced the Conductor pointing out the window, "your attention please. Behold . . . the northern lights!" He swept his arm across the huge sky, presenting the night like a circus ringmaster introducing a trapeze act.

As if he had called it to life, a giant curtain of colored light began to wave in the sky. The bottom of the aurora became deep red as it rippled faster, and then blue and purple waves appeared. The children were awestruck.

Suddenly bright points of light appeared, blinking so rapidly that they seemed to sizzle. They began to swirl, faster and faster, like a pinwheel the size of Wyoming — faster and brighter, brighter and faster. When everything dissolved to a soft green, and then finally faded away, the kids burst into applause.

The Polar Express was crossing a barren desert of ice. "And now," said the Conductor, "if you will be so kind as to direct your attention to the front of the train, to about 11 or 12 o'clock — 11:55 to be exact . . ." The kids craned their necks to look in that direction, as the Conductor's voice filled with reverence. "Those lights in the distance? Like the lights of a *s*trange ocean liner sailing on a frozen sea?"

The kids pointed excitedly.

"Ladies and gentlemen," the Conductor concluded, "*There* . . . is the North Pole!"

As the kids let out loud cheers, the Boy stared in wide-eyed wonder. So did the Girl.

The Polar Express thundered across a red brick trestle that rose right out of the ice. In the distance was a huge city, standing alone at the top of the world, large and imposing but also warm and inviting.

In North Pole City, hundreds of red brick factory buildings towered above frozen canals. Every building's eaves and gables were decorated with Christmas lights. The city seemed completely deserted. Not an elf was in sight.

The Polar Express rumbled slowly past the gigantic clock-tower entrance, where the clock above the entry arch read exactly 11:55.

The Conductor checked his pocket watch as well. "Five minutes till midnight. We just made it." He plopped down onto one of the seats and wiped his brow in relief. "Whew. That was what I call a close shave."

The Girl, who had been peering out the window, turned to the Conductor. She looked very concerned. "The elves! Where are the elves?" she wanted to know.

"Gathering at the center of the city," the Conductor explained. "Where one of you lucky children will receive the first gift of Christmas."

"Who gets the first gift of Christmas?" asked the Know-It-All.

"He will choose one of you," the Conductor replied, motioning toward the Boy.

The Girl stared pointedly at the Know-It-All. "Straight As, huh?" she said.

The Know-It-All was completely flummoxed. "It's not possible, it's —"

"Elves!" cried the boy with the missing teeth. The children were all glued to the windows, eyes wide.

They were elves, all right, thousands of tiny figures marching through the streets. They stood about eighteen inches tall and had pointed ears and pointed toes. Each one wore the same uniform: red tunic, green leotard, stocking cap trimmed in white fur. The elves paraded snappily to "O Tannenbaum," which was playing over the city's public address system. The streets were so crowded with Santa's helpers that the train could move no farther.

With a final *Sssssss* the Polar Express stopped.

The Conductor began escorting the children off the train. Up ahead, the elves were backing brightly colored circus wagons, towed by miniature steam-powered snowmobiles, up to the forward cars. Other elves immediately began unloading the broken toys.

Out of their minds with excitement, the children gathered in a group behind the Conductor. He checked the tower clock: 11:55. "Five minutes to midnight," he said. "Let's not dilly-dally."

The Know-It-All pushed to the front. "Hey! What gives? It was five till midnight four minutes ago."

"Exactly!" said the Conductor cheerfully. That put a cork into the Know-It-All. Glancing into the train, the Girl spotted the Lonely Boy, still sitting in the observation car. "What about him?" she asked urgently, tugging on the Conductor's coat.

The Conductor peered over his glasses. "He's decided to stay on the train," he observed. "No one is *required* to see Santa."

As they kept marching along behind the Conductor, the Boy and the Girl looked back at the Lonely Boy, and then back to each other.

"Come on!" the Girl said when she could stand it no longer.

"Are you — ?" started the Boy, about to ask if she was sure.

But she cut him off. "Don't ask!" she said.

As they ran back to the observation car, the Know-It-All spotted them sneaking off.

When they got to the car, the Boy gave the Girl a boost up the snow-caked stairs. When she got to the top, she reached down to help the Boy, but he slipped. His foot swung wide and caught on a lever. His weight on the lever lifted the pin, and the frozen slush caused the pin to stick in the retracted position. The Boy and Girl scrambled up the stairs without noticing any of this.

Inside the observation car, the Girl marched purposefully up to the Lonely Boy. "Look," she said with great certainty. "You have to come with us."

The Boy stepped forward. "She's right," he said.

The Lonely Boy slowly lifted his head and spoke softly: "Christmas just doesn't work out for me, never has."

"But Christmas is such a wonderful, beautiful, special time," the Girl pleaded. "It's a time for giving, and being thankful, and for friends and family, and everyone puts up decorations and lights, and Santa comes and leaves presents under our Christmas trees!"

"I've never had a Christmas tree," said the Lonely Boy.

The Boy and the Girl exchanged a stricken look. This was serious. This was sad.

"Christmas isn't for me," the Lonely Boy whispered.

"Look," said the Boy resolutely. "I don't know if Christmas is gonna work out for you, or if you'll ever have a Christmas tree, or presents. But I do know, you can't stay here by yourself."

"Yes! Come with us! We'll go together," the Girl chimed in.

The Lonely Boy looked up at his two new friends. He smiled for the first time. They smiled back.

Suddenly the car began to shudder and rumble. Because of the stuck pin an air hose broke open with a snakelike hiss and the car started moving.

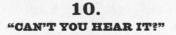

HE three children ran to the forward door and flung it open, only to find that the observation car was rolling backward. The rest of the Polar Express, the Conductor, the elves, and the kids were receding into the distance, and no one saw the car leaving. They were picking up speed. The three dashed out onto the rear platform, which was now the front of the car. The runaway car was rolling down the center of the street on the tracks. Moving even faster now, they rumbled around a turn. Ahead was a fork in the street. To the right was a gentle upward incline, to the left a steep drop. The tracks ran to the right, up the incline. "We're gonna be okay!" yelled the Boy.

At that moment a gust of wind howled through

the street. It blew snow off the cobblestones, revealing a switch track and a set of tracks heading to the left — downhill!

"Hold on!" the Boy hollered.

The three friends grabbed onto the railing as the observation car hit the switch track and lurched violently to the left. They were headed down the drop, and it was a nasty one. The runaway car screamed through the empty streets, speeding down the steep hills.

The car hit the bottom of a hill and rocketed down a long, narrow street. Ahead was a tunnel that was built right into the wall of a factory building.

"Uh-oh," said the Girl.

"Wait! The emergency brake!" said the Boy, remembering. He ran, pulled it — and nothing happened. "It doesn't work!" he cried.

At that instant, the car flew into the tunnel and the power was cut off. And then the Boy saw the King, hanging upside down on the outside of the car. Using his tin cup to bang on the window, he was pointing toward the front platform and mouthing some words: "A break, kid, take a break."

The Boy ran out onto the front platform, and there was the hobo, once again banging his cup.

This time he was whacking the manual brake wheel, mounted on the side of the car. The Boy grabbed the wheel, which was lit only by sparks. He pulled with all he had.

Skreeeeeeeeeeeee! The brake shoes began to grab, and the observation car slowed — but not enough, because now there were bright lights outside, and the car was heading right toward them. The Boy stared at the lights as they closed in. When he saw, looming just ahead, an enormous red car bumper with a great flashing red light on top, the Boy decided it was time to dive inside the car.

With a crash, the car jolted to a stop. The kids were thrown to the floor. Outside, everything was spinning. The Boy tried to stand but lost his balance and fell against a seat. Gradually, he realized that it was the observation car itself that was spinning.

The spinning slowed, and the three kids were able to stand up. They stumbled dizzily out of the car. Looking around, they found themselves in an immense round space, enclosed in a huge glass-paneled dome, like a greenhouse for giants. Garlands of twinkling Christmas lights hung everywhere. It was awesome.

In the center of this round space was a turntable that was used to reverse train cars. The observation car sat in the middle of the still-revolving turntable, its rear coupler wedged firmly against the bumper of another train car. Slowly, the turntable came to a stop.

Now there was a new problem, however. Seven track spurs radiated out from the platform like wheel spokes, and each track spur entered the mouth of a different tunnel. All seven tunnel entrances looked exactly the same.

"Now what?" said the Boy.

The Girl shook her head.

"It's my fault," the Lonely Boy said.

"No it isn't," replied the Boy.

"Because of me we're lost."

"Listen!" interrupted the Girl. "Hear that?"

The two boys strained to hear. Nothing.

"That bell!" said the Girl.

"Bell? What bell?" said the Boy.

"A sleigh bell," she said. "Can't you hear it?"

No, they couldn't.

The Girl pointed to one of the tunnels. "It's coming from that tunnel. That's the way we should go," she said firmly. "Come on!" She ran toward the entrance with the two boys following her. She tightrope-walked along the train tracks, crossing over a very deep, icy gorge below.

Finally they saw the end ahead of them.

Sprinting for it, they passed out of the darkness and into the bright moonlight.

They found themselves in a small square. Everything was elf-sized — the buildings, the curbs, the lampposts, all of it. At the center of the square, the tracks abruptly ended. Three narrow streets led out of the square. The three children stood there in the middle of the square, unsure which way to go.

The Girl stood quietly. She listened for a moment. Then she closed her eyes. "Yes," she whispered. "Yes." Eyes still closed, she continued to listen intently. "There it is! I hear it!" She pointed down one of the three streets.

"I don't hear anything!" the Boy said.

"This way!" she insisted, running.

"Are you sure?" said the Boy.

The Girl stopped dead in her tracks. She turned around slowly. Her eyes narrowed with conviction, and she spoke very deliberately.

"Yes."

She walked down the little street without looking back. The Lonely Boy followed her.

The Boy could do nothing but run after them. "Wait up!" he cried.

The three kids ran down the strange, snow-covered street. It snaked, turned, and zigzagged in all directions. There were no doors, no interesting lanes, only second-story windows too high up to see into.

At the end of the street was a narrow, walled staircase made of cobblestone, heading down. After hesitating at the top for a moment, the Girl started down, with the other two behind her.

At the bottom of the steep staircase was a narrow alley, and at the far end of that, a dead end. It looked as if it was as dead as a dead end could be, too: no openings, no doors, only high walls open to the sky, four stories above. A fine snow fluttered down.

The Girl couldn't believe it. "I was so sure . . ." she faltered.

"We'll have to go back the way we came," said the Boy. "But we'll never make it in time."

"I knew it," said the Lonely Boy quietly.

The Girl stopped him and looked right into his face. "I heard it," she told him. "I did. You just have to listen."

The Lonely Boy stared at her. Then he turned away, waiting to hear something. Dejected, the Girl started to walk on, but he did not move. He wanted so badly to believe his new friend was right.

Then his face changed. "I . . . I hear a bell," he said.

"A sleigh bell?" she asked.

The Lonely Boy nodded and pointed down the alley to the dead end. "It's coming from down there," he said.

The Girl came back to stand beside him, listened hard, then broke into a wide smile. "I hear it, too!" she said.

"I *don't,*" said the Boy, wild with frustration.

"Shhhhh," went the Girl, putting her finger to her lips.

"There's nothing to hear, that's why," said the Boy. "There's nothing back there. Come on, this is the only way out."

But the Lonely Boy was already walking slowly down the narrow gangway. The Girl followed.

Once again the Boy was left behind, frustrated, left out, having to follow on faith alone. Again he ran to catch up.

As the Lonely Boy moved toward the dead end, something amazing happened. There in front of him was a low wall, where no wall could be seen before. Looking down the alley from the bottom of the staircase, the walls had looked perfectly lined up. But when the angle changed, the low wall appeared. It was a cleverly done trick of the eye. There was a way out.

When the Boy caught up with them, he was

able to see what they could see: another stone stairway right behind the low wall, leading down to an underground hallway. A bright light shone at the bottom of the stairs.

"The bell's down there," said the Lonely Boy.

"How come *I* can't hear it?" cried the Boy.

"Let's go!" said the Girl.

The kids tiptoed down the stairs. At the bottom was the entrance to a wide tunnel. Quietly, they crept through it until they reached the end.

They found themselves on a viewing balcony, high above a massive eight-sided control room. Over the center of the room hung an octagonal, four-story bank of surveillance monitors, with thousands of small round TV screens. Most of them showed children asleep in bed.

In front of the monitors were long control panels. Five elves managed the entire operation. They wore telephone-operator headsets as they paced up and down, keeping a close watch on the monitors. The outside walls were lined with vintage Teletype machines. Reams of rolled paper had spilled out of each one, but now they all stood quiet.

Overhead, huge clocks displayed the time in cities all over the world. They all read 11:55.

A phone rang, and an elf answered it. Up

above, the three kids, careful not to make a sound, peeked over the balcony.

After putting down the phone, the elf went to his superior, an elf general with gold epaulets on his shoulders. "That was the Wrapping Hall, Chief," the elf reported.

"They just finished the last one," replied the general, checking his clipboard. "It's wrapped in Candy-Striped Red with a Number Seven Holly Green bow. What's the routing?"

Now the first elf checked his clipboard. "Goin' to the States," he said. "Grand Rapids, Michigan."

A loud horn hooted, making the kids jump. Red indicators on the control board lit up. *NAUGHTY ALERT*, they said. The Teletype chattered to life, and the lieutenant ran over to it and began reading the message.

"Apparently," he said, "a kid from Maplewood, New Jersey, just stuck some gum in his sister's hair."

"New Jersey?" said the general, perking up. "Is that the same kid who put the tack on his teacher's chair?"

The lieutenant checked the printout. "No, sir, this kid's name is . . . Steven."

The three kids in the balcony were mesmerized. So *that* was how Santa knew.

"So what do we do, Chief?" the lieutenant asked. "Alert the Big Man? We talking nuttin' for Christmas here?"

The general picked up the Hot Line, a big phone painted in red and white candy-cane stripes. He paused, and then looked up at the clocks. "Nah," he said. "It's almost Christmas. We'll cut him a break. But put him on the Check Twice list for next year."

The lieutenant picked up a clipboard and made a note, and the general put the phone down.

"All right, boys," he announced, "that's all for this year. Let's shut her down."

The elves began to throw switches. Indicator lights went off, and all the monitors went dark. The general walked toward a strange torpedo-shaped canister that sat in a clear pipe about four feet in diameter. The pipe passed through the far wall of the room. He opened a hatch in the little car and climbed in.

The rest of the elves finished shutting down the surveillance equipment and piled in behind the general. They closed the hatch, and — *sshhuuu-upt!* The car was sucked through the tube, as though it were in a giant vacuum cleaner hose.

The three kids were completely amazed, as

they stood on the balcony and looked down at the empty room.

Sshhuuuupt . . . an empty canister arrived. The three kids looked at one another. They knew what they had to do.

11.

THE canister hatch opened with a hiss of air. Inside, the seating was arranged like a bobsled, but upholstered in red leather and trimmed with shiny brass trim. The Girl climbed in the front, the Lonely Boy behind her, and the Boy in the rear.

The sled's nose was bullet-shaped and made of glass. There was a small instrument panel in front with three green buttons on it. Nothing was labeled, and the Girl had no idea which button to press. She closed her eyes and passed her hand over the buttons as if she were feeling their vibrations, whispering to herself: "Yes . . . yes . . ."

The Boy was getting irritated by all of this hocus-pocus. "Yes . . . *what?*" he burst out.

The Girl turned and looked the Boy right in the eye. "Yes . . . I believe."

She turned back and continued passing her hands over the buttons.

"There!" said the Lonely Boy. The Girl's finger paused over the middle button.

"What?" the Boy repeated, feeling mystified and shut out.

Now the Girl was hearing what the Lonely Boy had heard. "The bell," she said.

"*What bell?*" said the Boy, at the end of his wits.

Without hesitation, the Girl pushed the middle button. The hatch slammed down. *Sshhuuuuuupt!* They were off!

They flew through the brass tube like a rocket, at speeds reaching over a hundred miles an hour as their path bent, dipped, curved, and corkscrewed. Rings of lights flashed past them, making the ride feel even faster.

The ride was over before they knew it, as the canister slid to a fast but smooth stop. But they did not seem to be where they were supposed to be. They had arrived in a huge glass building, many times bigger than the one they'd just been in, with not a soul in it. It was dead quiet.

The tube hatch popped up. The Girl tried

pressing all the buttons on the instrument panel, but nothing happened.

"Maybe there's another way out," said the Boy, hopping out of the canister to have a look around.

The entire place was decorated with Christmas lights, wreaths, and garlands. A giant conveyor belt ran past wrapping stations with huge rolls of ribbon and wrapping paper hanging above each workbench. This was the Great Gift-Wrapping Hall.

The Girl and the Lonely Boy climbed out and walked around the hall with the Boy. The floor was covered waist-deep in gift-wrap trimmings. The conveyor belts sat still and empty.

This time the Boy led the way. They climbed onto one of the conveyor belts and started to run along it. Pretty soon they found themselves in a new room, also huge. This was the Sorting Hall. It was a maze of chutes, slides, and conveyor belts. There were no doors, no windows, only the sorting machinery, also silent and still. The Lonely Boy and the Girl looked at each other expectantly, still hoping to hear the bell.

They didn't, and the Boy was out of ideas too. "We're going to miss everything," said the Girl hopelessly.

It made them so sad, to have come so far for nothing.

And then, with a loud buzz, a conveyor belt in the center of the room started up, then a second, then a third.

"Look!" cried the Boy.

A solitary present was chugging toward them on the conveyor belt, wrapped in candy-striped red. As it passed in front of the Boy, he glanced at the parchment routing slip. "Hey! It's going to my town," he said. He lifted the attached gift tag to read it. "To somebody named Billy," he said.

Lonely Boy perked up. "My — *my* name is Billy," he said, not daring to hope.

The gift dropped from the first belt to an intersecting one below it and rolled past the Girl. She read the routing slip aloud as it went by: "11344 Edbrooke Ave."

"That's my address!" Billy yelled.

The Boy and the Girl were as surprised as he was. But the present was still moving, heading toward a hole in the wall at the far end of the belt. In a few seconds it would disappear. Billy took off after it. There was no way he was going to let his precious present get away.

When the present was just inches from the

hole, Billy dove onto the conveyor belt, grabbed the box just as it slipped past the leather flap, and held on for dear life. The Christmas gift disappeared though the hole, and so did Billy.

The Boy and Girl exchanged one quick look, then jumped onto the conveyor belt. Sprinting toward the hole, they dove through it after Billy.

Immediately they found themselves sliding down a huge, polished stainless-steel chute.

The chute was inside a building as large as an airplane hangar, woven together with dozens of similar chutes, like a tower of spaghetti, all dropping hundreds of feet. Sliding down the chute, the Boy caught occasional glimpses of Billy, who was weaving and bobbing several yards ahead.

The chute dumped the Boy and the Girl into a huge, polished funnel. Just ahead of them Billy slid and swooped along the funnel's gleaming walls, still hanging onto his Christmas present.

The three of them spiraled faster and faster, down into the vortex, until they were swept into the hole in the center and dropped straight down — onto the largest pile of Christmas presents imaginable. It was literally a mountain of gifts of every shape and size, each beautifully wrapped and beribboned.

When they all bobbed up to the surface of this

ocean of gifts, Billy still had a viselike grip on his present, and he sported an ear-to-ear grin. "Look!" he said, holding up the gift tag so his friends could see it.

" 'Merry Christmas, Billy,' " the Girl read, her eyes going moist. "'From Mr. C.'"

Billy shook the present. "I think I know what it is!" he said. "I've wanted one of these my whole life!" He reached for the corner of the wrapping paper, about to rip it open.

"Wait!" said the Girl. She pointed to another tag taped to the box: Do not open until Christmas.

Billy looked questioningly at the Boy. Could this be true? Was it some kind of cruel joke?

"Those are the rules," said the Boy.

Then they heard the loud whir of a motor somewhere overhead, and a large shadow moved toward them from above. Overhead, they could see a large painted bullseye, its center open to the night sky. The motor sound stopped. There was a long silence.

Crack! Crack! Crack! Fffsssizzzz! Skyrockets!

From the outer corners of the gift mountain, four rockets suddenly shot upward. They sizzled upward, each trailing a long rope, and disappeared through the hole, pulling the four ropes taut behind them.

Now the roaring sound of aircraft engines was directly overhead. The ropes continued to be pulled up, lifting large sections of burlap material up around the mountain of gifts. Very soon, the gifts and the three children were enclosed in a gigantic scratchy brown sack, which got tighter and tighter around them as it was hauled upward. The gifts rumbled and shifted as the kids clambered up the presents, trying to get to the mouth of the sack.

The skylight parted in the middle and its halves pulled apart, opening the ceiling up to the night sky. The kids stared in amazement through the snow that swirled in above them.

The gigantic sack was hanging from an enormous zeppelin, an airship larger than the *Titanic*. It was painted with colorful stripes and festooned with blinking Christmas lights. Its propellers roared loudly as it maneuvered into position to pull the giant sack up through the skylight and into the night sky. Attached to the airship's keel was a vast aluminum rigging, and riding on the struts of this rigging, right out in the open, were hundreds of elves.

"Come on!" the Girl yelled to her friends as she began piling up presents as fast as she could. It took the boys only a moment to get it: she was making a ladder!

They could feel themselves being drawn higher

and higher into the air. Meanwhile, they kept piling up gifts against the side of the sack until they could cautiously climb the shaky pile. At last they were at the opening, peering over the lip of the sack. Billy was still clinging to his special present.

The view was spectacular. They were floating low above North Pole City, barely clearing the rooftops and chimneys. The zeppelin, enormous above them, floated at a smooth, stately pace.

Suddenly Billy lost his footing and started to sink into the gift pile, as though into quicksand. "Something's got me!" he yelled, terrified.

His friends reached for Billy's free arm. They tried to tug him up by the wrist, but it was no good. "It's got my leg!" he cried.

"I can't hold him!" said the Girl through gritted teeth.

"Give us your other hand," the Boy called down to him.

The Boy and Girl strained, but with a hold on only one of Billy's hands, they couldn't get the leverage they needed. He was going under. With their last strength, they gave one final heave, and Billy slowly emerged from the sea of gifts. Breathing hard, he struggled to the top of the pile.

Holding on to Billy's ankle was a hand — a child's hand.

They kept pulling, and the Know-It-All appeared, his hand clinging onto Billy's foot.

"What are *you* doing here?" the Girl demanded.

"Same as you!" he retorted. "Checking on my Christmas presents. I wanna make sure I'm gettin' everything on my list."

"Look!" interrupted the Boy, pointing down below. The kids scrambled to peek over the lip of the sack.

A quarter mile below them was the main square of the city. Thousands of elves stood shoulder to shoulder, packing the great square wall to wall. And there was the Polar Express, engulfed in the sea of elves.

In the exact center of the square was a large clear area marked by an inlaid marble compass rose, just like the ones they had seen on maps. Except on this compass rose, being that it was at the North Pole, all four arrows pointed south.

The kids in the sack heard a calm, neutral elf voice over the public address system. "You may start your descent any time now," said the elf air traffic controller. "At your convenience, of course."

PPFFFFffffffttt! The zeppelin crew began releasing helium from the airship, and it began a controlled descent.

The Girl pointed to the clock tower. "Look, it's still five to," she said. "We're gonna make it."

"Of course we will," said the Know-It-All. "We got plenty of time. Nothing but time. We got time to kill."

The zeppelin continued to descend, dropping lower and lower. Maybe too low.

"You know what?" said the Boy. "I don't think we're gonna make it."

He had called it right. The sack was hanging too low, and the four children were headed straight for a gigantic five-pointed star on top of the Christmas tree that was at the center of North Pole City.

"Altitude, please, a bit more altitude, please," said the elf air traffic controller in the same calm voice.

He was the only one who was calm, however. Thousands of elves now began screaming and pointing to the sky. *Look out! Look out!*

The zeppelin's engines immediately were thrown into reverse, but the sack was headed right for the pointy star.

"Up, please," said the unflappable voice on the loudspeaker. Meanwhile, four dozen elves swan-dived off the zeppelin rigging, yelling, "Geronimo!" in their tiny voices as they fell.

Lighter now, the zeppelin began to gain altitude. The elf skydivers gave the kids curious looks as they plummeted past.

"Two cubits more, if you please!" the voice requested.

Another group of elves jumped, joining hands to form an aerial star formation.

The four kids craned their necks to see.

Pop! Pop! Tiny, brightly colored parachutes blossomed open when the jumpers were about a hundred feet from the ground. The elves floated safely into the square, each making a perfect ground-roll landing.

The kids sighed with relief, but not for long. The sack was still not going to clear the star! The bottom of the sack snagged on one of the star's points, tipping it over and dragging it off the tree.

The crowd below gasped and scattered in all directions as the huge star plummeted to the ground. But in his rush to escape, one little elf lost his footing, tripped, and went sprawling to the ground — exactly in the path of the falling star.

Instantly, three more elves dove off the zeppelin's rigging. But these elves were not parachutists. These elves were harnessed to a bungee cord!

The special squad bungee-dove toward the

plunging star, and snatched it out of the air at the exact second that it gently grazed the nose of the terrified elf on the ground. All the elves in the square clapped and cheered.

Clear of the tree now, the zeppelin released some more helium. The sack descended, maneuvering perfectly toward the compass-rose landing pad. Some of the elves on the ground climbed on top of one another's shoulders, creating little pyramids five elves high. As the zeppelin descended, the highest elves grabbed onto the sack and pulled it down. Others were jumping on mini-trampolines and pogo sticks so they could bounce up and latch onto the sack as well.

As the sack touched down, a platoon of elves rappelled down from the airship to disconnect the sack from the ship.

"Good-bye," said the calm voice on the loud-speaker.

This was the cue for all of the elves left on the zeppelin rigging to jump. The zeppelin, light as a feather now, rose quickly into the air.

The free-falling elves put on a spectacular skydiving show, performing somersaults, twists, jackknives, tucks, and full gainers to the wild applause of the spectators below. From their perch at the lip of the sack, the four kids watched in amazement.

But now the jig was up. Three elves appeared at the mouth of the sack and looked in at them. "A'right, youse stowaways . . . party's over," said one of them.

12.
SANTA CLAUS IS COMING TO TOWN

THE Know-It-All immediately pointed to the other three kids. "I just followed them," he said.

"We fell in here by mistake," the Boy tried.

"Aaw, figgidaboudit," said the elf. "We knew yas was in dere da whole time." The elves helped the kids climb to the edge of the bag.

Whoops. The sack stood thirty feet off the ground. The four kids gulped.

"So's dat nobody gets hoit," said the elf, "here's how we're gonna git youse down."

The Know-It-All butted to the front of the line and interrupted the elf with a cocky air. "It's simple!" he said. "I know —"

"Whadda *you* know?" returned the elf. "You're not supposed to be here in the first place. But I tell you what. Since it's Christmas I'm gonna let you . . . slide." He grinned devilishly. "Going down!" he announced, kicking the burlap so that the edge caved in.

Whoosh! The Know-It-All dropped onto his butt and slid down the side of the sack, screaming all the way, until two elves caught him easily at the bottom. The Conductor and the other kids from the train were waiting down there, too.

Now it was Billy's turn. He still clung to his present, but the elf reached for it. "We'll hold onta dis for ya," he said.

Billy didn't want to let go.

"It's in safe hands," the elf said, giving Billy a reassuring wink. "Trust me."

The Elf gently took the box, and Billy slid down, to be caught at the bottom by the Conductor and the Know-It-All.

Whoosh! Down came the Girl.

Whoosh! Down came the Boy.

The Conductor took out his watch and stared pointedly at the Boy. "Cutting it a little tight, aren't we?"

He nodded toward the center of the square. The Boy gasped when he saw what the Conductor was looking at. There, on a raised stone platform, stood a wonderful, glorious thing, something the Boy had thought he would never ever see. It was Santa's sleigh. It was enormous, beautifully made, and polished till it shone.

Like ants walking off with a picnic, hundreds of elves lifted the giant sack above their heads and carried it to Santa's sleigh.

At the sound of a trumpet fanfare, eight reindeer were led into the square, each wearing a shiny leather harness.

A second fanfare sounded, and forty elves, in two lines, carried two decorative gold harnesses into the square. Each one was bedecked with silver jingle bells. As the elves marched through the square, they raised the harnesses above their heads and shook them.

The elves and the children cheered, but the Boy was silent. He had heard nothing from the bells.

The elves gave the bells another exuberant shake as the crowd cheered. The Girl turned to the Boy, giddy with excitement. "Isn't that the most beautiful sound?" she said.

The Boy could not respond. He had turned very pale, and felt sick to his stomach. *Why* couldn't he hear the bells?

Now came the loudest trumpet fanfare of all.

All the elves turned toward the clock tower and began to sing:

> *You better watch out,*
> *You better not cry . . .*

Thousands of elves were singing in unison, and the sound was like nothing the children had ever heard before. All those tiny elf voices together sounded weird, beautiful, and haunting.

> *You better not pout,*
> *I'm telling you why . . .*
> *SANTA CLAUS IS COMING TO*
> *TOWNNNN!!*

This last verse was followed by more cheering and wild applause. The sea of elves parted, clearing a path from the clock tower to the sleigh. The Boy, still shaken and pale, looked toward the clock tower. In the tower archway he saw a flash of red, but it was obliterated by elves excitedly waving their arms. Then he got a glimpse of the very top of the hat. It was instantly blocked by the children jumping up and down.

The Girl was beside herself with joy. "He's here! He's here!" she was screaming.

"I see him!" yelled Billy.

A loud clatter erupted from the reindeer as they saw Santa. They pranced and hovered frantically, pulling and snapping at their bridles.

At that moment, a solitary jingle bell popped off one of the gold harnesses. It sailed high into the air, seeming to move in slow motion, and its downward arc led straight to the Boy.

It made no sound as it slowly bounced on the cobblestones and rolled right up to the Boy's foot. He blinked a few times. No one else seemed to have seen, for all eyes were elsewhere. He bent down and picked up the bell.

It was the most beautiful bell he'd ever seen. He shook it, hoping to hear something, but there was no sound at all.

The Boy looked at the bell for a long moment. Then he closed his eyes as tightly as he could. "Yes . . . yes . . ." he whispered. With his eyes still closed, he gave the bell a small, thoughtful shake. "I believe," he said.

Ting . . . a-ling!

And there it was. The note was wonderful. It was amazing. It was glorious. It was the most beautiful bell sound in the whole wide world.

The Boy opened his eyes to find, reflected in its perfectly polished finish — *Santa*.

The Boy's jaw dropped, and he slowly turned to see the Big Man in all his yuletide glory. He stood above the Boy, with a smile as warm as the sun on his face. The Boy remembered the line from the old poem: "His eyes, how they twinkled! His dimples how merry!" Santa really did look like that.

Santa bent down to the open-mouthed Boy, that famous twinkle in his eye. "What was that you said?" he asked in a rich, deep voice.

The Boy slowly held up the bell. "I . . . I believe . . . believe this is yours," he said. Santa took the jingle bell in his spotless fur mitten. "Why, thank you," he said. "Ho, ho, ho." His round belly shook like a bowl full of jelly.

The Know-It-All tugged at Santa's sleeve. "Me! Me! Pick me!" he pestered.

The Girl, incredulous, pulled his arm away. "What are you doing? Stop it!" she cried.

But the Know-It-All put his hand right back on Santa's sleeve. "Pick me for the first gift!" he insisted.

Santa turned, his twinkling eyes finding the Know-It-All. "Patience, young man," he said. "You don't get it by asking." The Know-It-All was struck dumb as Santa looked into his eyes in a commanding but gentle way. "And a smidgen of humility might also serve you well," Santa added.

The Know-It-All lowered his arm. He looked as if he were shrinking. "Yes, sir," he said meekly.

Santa turned to the Girl. "And you, young lady," he said as she stared at him awestruck, "a girl of decision, full of confidence and spirit — Christmas Spirit that is — Ho! Ho! Ho!" he laughed at his own joke. "Keep up the good work."

The Girl smiled at Santa and nodded. She would, of course she would. She just couldn't talk.

Now Santa rested his great calming hand on Billy's shoulder. "And, Billy . . . it is Billy?"

Billy nodded.

"I see you've made some new friends," Santa said to him.

Billy looked over toward the Boy and the Girl. "Yes, sir," he said, full of pride. "I sure have."

"Well done, lad. There is no greater gift than friendship."

Now Santa raised his arms, and in his booming voice addressed the multitudes. "And speaking of gifts," he said, pointing his mittens right at the Boy, "let's have this fellow right here!"

The Boy gulped, utterly stunned.

The Conductor gave the Boy a knowing wink. He had known all along!

Santa hopped up onto his sleigh. Then the Conductor helped the Boy onto Santa's huge knee.

This was *not* like the department store. "Now," said Santa, "what would you like for Christmas?"

"Me?" said the Boy, still in shock.

"You."

The Boy pondered this question for a long moment. He looked over at the Girl and Billy, then at the Conductor. Everyone in the square fell silent.

Then the Boy leaned over and whispered in Santa's ear. Santa smiled that big warm smile.

"Yes, indeed," he said, "yes, *indeed*."

Santa stood in his sleigh, and with great dramatic flair, he lifted the single silver bell high above his head. "The first gift of Christmas!" he declared.

The elves roared their approval as Santa leaned and spoke to the Boy. "This bell," he said quietly, "is a wonderful symbol of the spirit of Christmas . . . as am I. But always remember, the true spirit of Christmas lies in your heart."

Santa patted his chest right where his heart was. Then he handed the Boy the bell.

The instant the bell touched the Boy's fingers . . . *bong!* The clock struck midnight. Everyone cheered. "Merry Christmas!" they all cried.

The Conductor sidled up to the Boy and pointed to the bell. "Better keep that in a safe place," he said over the din of the crowd.

The Boy immediately put the bell into his robe pocket, and the Conductor helped him down from the sleigh. The reindeer handlers let go of their charges. With a final push from the elves, the present-laden sleigh lifted off.

High above the square soared the sleigh and reindeer. They could still hear Santa whistle and shout: "Now, Dasher! Now, Dancer! Now, Prancer and Vixen! On, Comet! On, Cupid! On, Donner and Blitzen!"

The Boy, Girl, Billy, and the rest of the children watched Santa's magical flight in wide-eyed wonder. "This is exactly how I dreamed it would be!" cried the Girl.

Suddenly worried, Billy leaned in close to the Boy. "Could all of this be nothing but a dream?" he asked.

The Boy looked him straight in the eye with unwavering conviction. "No," he said.

Santa's sleigh zoomed overhead one last time, and they all heard his deep voice: "To the top of the porch! To the top of the wall! Now dash away! Dash away! Dash away all!" He gave his whip a final crack, and the sleigh vanished, leaving behind a rainbow-colored trail of fairy dust.

The elves stopped singing and stared at the sky in silence, as if they had just witnessed a miracle, which of course they had. It was no less miraculous for happening every year.

Then they shouted and tossed their pointy elf caps into the air. And as the hats fell with the gentle snow, the Boy noticed for the first time that half the elves were bald and the other half had ponytails. They were girl elves!

Now the Conductor turned to the children. "All aboard!" he called.

The stone platform that held Santa's sleigh began to rise out of the ground beneath it. It formed a stage upon which was an elf rock-and-roll band, playing a great version of "Jingle Bell Rock." All the elves began jitterbugging with each other in the street. The children from the train were lost in a vast North Pole party.

Two little elves were not celebrating, though. They were busy doing the last job, working with all their strength to pump a handcar up the track back in the square. The handcar was pushing the runaway observation car back to the Polar Express. Then the two elves collapsed, exhausted. The Polar Express was now ready to roll.

13.
TICKETS

S the children lined up, waiting to board the train, the Conductor stood at the bottom of the passenger car steps, checking tickets.

The Know-It-All handed his over, and the Conductor punched some more letters on it before handing it back. The Know-It-All glanced at it, surprised. Now the letters spelled something. "LEAN," he read. "Whatever that's supposed to mean?"

The Conductor looked the ticket over. "I believe 'LEAN' is spelled with only four letters," he said. "I'd say there were five there."

The Know-It-All angrily snatched the ticket back. "Are you saying I don't know how to —" he began, but caught himself as he looked at the ticket more closely. "Oh, it says 'LEARN.' I'm sorry . . . my mistake."

The Conductor smiled, happy to see a smidgen of humility at last. "Well done. Lesson learned," he said, and waved him on board.

Billy was next in line. "Ticket?" the Conductor inquired.

Billy handed his over with pleasure, and the Conductor punched another letter onto it. It now spelled ON.

"Needs a bit more," said the Conductor. He punched some more letters and handed it back to Billy.

Billy stared at it and, as he did, it kept changing before his eyes. First it read DEPEND ON, then LEAN ON, then COUNT ON.

"That's some special ticket," he said proudly.

"So," said the Conductor, "can you count on us to get you home, safe and sound?"

"Absolutely," Billy replied. He turned and smiled at the Girl and the Boy. "Me . . . and my friends," he added.

The Conductor smiled as Billy boarded the train. "Next!" he said.

Now the Girl handed the Conductor her ticket, looking expectant. What would hers say? The Conductor punched it and handed it back. She read it, a confused look spreading over her face. "It spells 'LEAD'? Like lead balloon?"

"Are you sure?" the Conductor asked, smiling.

This was the question that got her every time. She looked at the ticket again.

"I believe," said the Conductor, "that could also spell 'lead,' as in *'leader.'* And *leadership*. And *lead the way*. If you want it to."

The Girl's answer was clear and strong. She was sure now. "I do," she said. "Yes. Lead."

The Conductor snapped to attention and gave the Girl a salute. "Follow you anywhere, ma'am," he said briskly.

The Girl broke into a big smile and proudly climbed the stairs.

The Boy was last in line. He stepped forward.

"Ah, yes," said the Conductor. "The boy with all the questions." Speedily, he punched the Boy's ticket — behind his back — and then handed it back to the Boy without even looking at it.

The Boy looked at the writing on his ticket. It clearly spelled BELIEVE. He started to tell the Conductor: "It says —"

The Conductor lifted his hand and stopped him. "Nothing I need to know," he said. He leaned in close to the Boy. "Only you do."

The Boy nodded. He understood now. He believed.

"All aboard!" called the Conductor, his eye twinkling.

The Boy stepped on. The Conductor signaled the engineer, bent down, and picked up the step.

Inside the passenger car, the Boy took a seat, and all the kids gathered around him. "Let's see it!" said the boy who was missing teeth.

"Let's see the bell!" the red-haired girl chimed in.

The Boy smiled and reached into his robe.

His face filled with horror as his fingers poked through the hole in the pocket. "It's gone!" he gasped.

The other kids looked serious, and tears began to well up in the Boy's eyes. "I lost it," he said bleakly. "I lost the bell from Santa's sleigh."

"Don't worry," said Billy with amazing confidence. "We'll find it."

"We'll help you . . . all of us," said the Know-It-All, with equally amazing sincerity.

The Girl jumped up. "Let's hurry outside and look for it," she said.

The others jumped up, ready to go, but at that moment, with a sharp lurch, the Polar Express started moving. They were on their way home.

The Boy sat down, heartbroken, and the other children were quiet, feeling sad for him. Slowly they drifted back to their own seats.

"That's really too bad," the Know-It-All said simply.

Even the steady *click-clack* of the train wheels sounded sad.

Like a toy train, the Polar Express circled beneath the giant Christmas tree in the square before departing. Outside, the elves still danced. But inside the train the mood was melancholy.

The Girl put her arm around the Boy. "I'm sorry," she said.

But the Boy was inconsolable. He lowered his head in sorrow. The kids sat with him silently.

It was going to be a long ride home.

The bright yellow beam from the headlight cut through the softly falling snow as the locomotive rumbled to a stop.

"11344 Edbrooke," the Conductor called out.

The Boy sat in the exact same spot he had occupied from the beginning, head bowed, heartbroken. The other children had been asleep, but now they began to stir.

"Next stop, 11344 Edbrooke," the Conductor announced again.

It was Billy's stop. He paused as he passed the

Boy, and he offered his hand. "Thank you," he said to the Boy. "For everything."

The Boy nodded and shook Billy's hand gravely.

Then the Girl took Billy's hand. "You have a wonderful Christmas," she said.

"You too," Billy replied. He smiled at his two new friends. "Well, gotta go," he said with reluctance.

As he stepped off the train, the Girl wiped a patch of frost off her window with her sleeve. "Look!" she said, nudging the Boy. He leaned over to look out of the clear spot.

In the front window of Billy's house was a small Christmas tree. Its modest lights twinkled brightly. Billy saw it too, leaped with glee, and ran at full blast into the house.

The Polar Express blew its whistle and began to pull out. The Girl and the Boy watched Billy's house start to disappear behind the falling snow.

Billy ran back out onto his front porch, holding the present — *his* present, the one with the red and white stripes. He held it proudly high above his head. Then he waved farewell to the train and the children.

"Santa already made it to Billy's house," said the Girl. "Amazing!"

The Boy nodded. He was happy for Billy, at least as happy as he could be at that moment.

In a few minutes, they had reached the Boy's house. The Boy, the Girl, and the Know-It-All walked out onto the car platform.

"I'm sorry about the bell," the Girl said. "It was a really special present."

The Boy nodded miserably. "I guess it's the thought that counts," Know-It-All said, without believing it. Then he turned and walked back into the passenger car.

"Yes. It is," the Boy said ruefully.

The Girl gave him a warm hug, and they looked at each other for a long moment. So much had happened, and they were so close now.

It was time to leave. "Watch your step," said the Conductor, all business as he helped the Boy down the steps. At the bottom, the Boy extended his hand.

"Thank you," he said.

The Conductor gave the Boy's hand a hearty shake. "You know . . ." he began after the Boy had turned to go.

The Boy turned back to hear.

"One thing about trains," said the Conductor. "It doesn't matter where they're going, what matters is deciding to get on." He gave the Boy a wink.

The Boy turned and trudged up the path to his house. On the train, all the children were waving, and the Boy was sad to leave. The Girl waved last, with that special smile of hers. The Boy waved back. The Conductor signaled the engine with his lantern, and the whistle blew.

The Boy stood in the front yard, looking at his house. It was dark inside, and the Christmas tree was just a big shadow in the corner. Reflected in the living room windows the lights of the Polar Express's passenger car shone brightly.

He opened the front door and went in, pausing in the doorway to take one last look back at the train. The pistons hissed. The train began to move. As the Conductor rolled past, he said something that the Boy couldn't hear.

"Whaaat?" yelled the Boy.

The Conductor cupped his hands around his mouth and shouted: "Merry Christmas!"

The Conductor waved good-bye and the Boy waved back. Then something caught the Boy's eye — a shape on top of the observation car. Could it be? The King? Sitting at his campfire? Waving his Santa Claus hat? That smile . . .

Then he vanished, swirling away with the smoke and the steam.

The Polar Express let out a long blast from the whistle . . . and was gone.

14.
WHEN CHRISTMAS COMES TO TOWN

THE Boy slowly closed the front door. He checked his pocket one last time, hoping for a miracle, but there was no bell. There was only the hole.

He looked around the living room. It was just as he'd left it: no gifts under the tree, empty stockings hanging on the mantel. Santa's cookies and milk were untouched.

The Boy slowly climbed the hall stairs and went to bed.

"Wake up!" Sarah shouted. "Wake up!"

The Boy's sleepy eyes fluttered open. Sarah stood beside his bed, shaking him. Daylight already filled his room. "Wake up!" she yelled again. "Santa's been here! Santa's been here!"

The second Sarah ran out of the room, the Boy jumped out of bed and ran straight to the window.

A fresh blanket of snow covered everything on his street. The sky was clear. There were no tracks, no ruts, not a hint that the Polar Express had rumbled through. There was only the snowman, standing guard.

"Hurry up!" Sarah called from downstairs.

As the Boy scrambled to put on his slippers, he noticed something peculiar. His clock was still stopped at 11:55.

He yanked his robe off the bedpost. *Rrriiipp!* There went the pocket. A couple of marbles rattled to the floor, just as they had before. How strange.

The Boy put his hand in the pocket, and his fingers slipped through. The hole felt exactly the way it had the night before.

Half an hour later, the living room floor was covered with torn wrapping paper, snarled ribbons, boxes and bows. And of course, toys.

Sarah was still rummaging around under the Christmas tree, and she found one last present, a small box wrapped in exactly the same striped paper as Billy's gift had been. "This one has your name on it," she said, handing it to the Boy.

Recognizing the paper, he ripped it off the present as fast as he could. Inside was a box. He opened it and peeked inside, as his heart pounded.

The Boy's jaw dropped. It was the silver bell.

He shook it, and it made the most beautiful sound in the world. Sarah shook it too. It sounded wonderful.

There was one more thing inside the box. It was a note, written on parchment. It read:

Found this on the seat of my sleigh. Better fix that hole in your pocket.

Mr. C.

The Boy smiled hugely. He could almost hear Santa's voice in his head as he read the note. He rang the bell once again. It was beautiful.

Their parents walked into the living room, wading through the discarded paper. "What a lovely bell," said Mom, seeing what her son was holding. "Who's it from?"

"Santa," said the Boy.

"Really," she said, smiling at his joke.

Proudly, the Boy handed her the bell. She lifted it to her ear, shook it, frowned, and tried it again.

"Oh . . . that's too bad," she said, disappointed by its silence.

The Boy and his sister exchanged a look. They'd certainly heard it.

Their mother handed the bell to their father. He held it close to his ear and gave it a shake. "Yes," he said. "It's broken. Sorry about that, Sport." He handed the bell back to the Boy, and he and Mom left the room.

When they were gone, the Boy rang the bell once again. It was glorious, just as before. He shared a knowing look with Sarah.

"Come on, kids. We'll be late for church!" their mother called from the foyer.

Sarah jumped up and ran off, but the Boy remained, cradling his treasure in his hands. He walked over to the coffee table and carefully set the bell down next to Santa's now empty milk glass. He could see his reflection in the polished silver. He gave the bell one last look before leaving.

Many years later, the Man remembered.

At one time most of his friends had been able to hear the bell too, but as the years passed, it fell silent for all of them. Even Sarah found one Christmas that she could no longer hear its sweet sound.

But it was not so for the Man. For him, even after he'd grown old, the bell still rang, as it does for all who truly believe.

Because of course, he had taken a trip on the Polar Express.